Romancing
the Rum Runner

Romancing the Rum Runner

MICHELLE MCLEAN

Entangled Publishing, LLC
2614 South Timberline Road
Suite 109
Fort Collins, CO 80525
Visit our website at www.entangledpublishing.com.

Scandalous is an imprint of Entangled Publishing, LLC.

Edited by Erin Molta
Cover design by Gwen Hayes and Heidi Stryker

Manufactured in the United States of America

First Edition June 2014

SCANDALOUS

To TCR, my love always

Chapter One

Jessica Harlan brought the cleaver down with enough force to sever the bone and then wiped her bloody hand on her apron. A small crowd gathered at her counter, a sight that would have warmed her heart if it wasn't for the presence of Jameson lurking in the corner.

"Agent Jameson," she called. "What can I help you with today?"

Jameson's eyebrow rose a notch as he cast a glance around her busy shop. "I can wait a moment. Go ahead and take care of your customers."

He smiled, though Jessie didn't buy it for a second. He tried to be charming but never quite pulled it off.

"Suit yourself." She turned back to the woman at the counter, trying to ignore the loathsome man.

Earl Jameson was particularly troublesome, even for a prohibition agent. He was the first prohi agent who seemed immune to bribes. The last one had left her alone, as long as he was allowed to confiscate a few bottles of her father's best gin every month. Bottles Jessie was fairly sure went straight down the man's gullet rather than into the sewer where they were supposed to go. But at least it had kept him out of her business.

She hadn't been so lucky with Jameson. His wardrobe was far too nice for him to be totally clean, but if he was taking bribes it wasn't from her. Maybe his family was wealthy, and the little weasel just liked to ruin people's lives. The man was determined to bring down the Phoenix, the mythical man Jessie had fabricated to run her speakeasy, The Red Phoenix. Having the Phoenix as her "boss" let her put a little distance between the speakeasy's owner and herself, and her employees did better thinking their boss was male.

Only Joe and her best friend—and best act—Maude, knew that she and the Phoenix were one and the same. The Feds, and most everyone else, assumed she was the Phoenix's moll. A girlfriend with a little more power than normal, sure. But nothing more than his public face. And that's the way Jessie liked to keep it.

Jameson made it a point to stop by once a week or so. He never bought anything. Just came in to chitchat. As if his presence alone would make her break down and confess everything. Jessie snorted. Jameson was a real potato and wasn't nearly as suave as he believed himself to be. And he'd never outsmart Jessie.

That didn't stop him from trying, though. The man was a nuisance, and one she wanted gone from her shop. His eyes on her made her skin crawl.

When another customer walked through the door to get in line behind the three already at the counter, Jameson tipped his hat at her. "Perhaps I'll return when you aren't so occupied."

"If you prefer," she said, bringing the cleaver down again, taking her frustration out on the poor chops beneath her blade.

He nodded and moved toward the door.

The tension in Jessie's shoulders ebbed and she quickly wrapped the two chops in butcher paper and handed them to the young woman who was waiting.

"There you are. That'll be eighty-two cents."

The young woman gave her a dollar and when Jessica handed her the change, the woman dropped a penny in the little dish on the counter and asked, "Is the cod fresh tonight?"

Jessica looked up, her full attention focused on her customer. She looked like she squared up all right. Jessie had a nose for people, whether or not they were good or bad, or a tattler or not. The woman in front of her looked a bit nervous, but in an, *oh my goodness I can't believe I'm doing this,* way. Not an, *I'm an undercover officer here to catch you,* way. Plus, the woman had known the correct pass phrase and gesture.

"No," Jessie answered. "But it'll be fresh tomorrow. Getting a new shipment in around midnight."

The woman gave her a shy smile and nodded. Then she clasped her meat to her chest and ran out of the store as fast as she politely could. Through the door held open by Jameson.

Jessie tensed. *Had he heard?* She forced her muscles to loosen. Even if he had, he couldn't know what it meant. Jameson nodded and finally took his sorry carcass out the door. Jessie tried to put him from her mind and took care of her remaining customers.

Joe came up behind her once the crowd had cleared out. "I don't like these kids coming in here. There's got to be a better way to get the word out about when the joint will be open for business. The Feds are going to get wise to this scheme one of these days. Surprised they haven't already."

"Well, even if they do, that's why we have the raid alarm. It's not like the Feds will be quiet when they show up. If we ever get raided, we should have plenty of time to get everyone out. The fact that we've never had to test it means our system is working. It's kept us safe so far, and there really isn't a better way of spreading the word. We can hardly tack up a flyer in the lobby.

"Besides, making them come inside to find out when The Red Phoenix will be open means more sales for us. They always buy something, and they spread the word themselves just enough that we aren't overrun. It's a good system. Don't be such a wet blanket," she said, shoving him playfully.

Joe shook his head and walked away, muttering under his breath. The old man was a dear, and had been helping out in her father's butcher shop for more years than Jessie had been alive. She hated to worry him, but really, she'd been over and over the safest way to keep her speakeasy up and running and the procedures she had in place had worked pretty well, so far. The Red Phoenix was the only speakeasy in Chicago she knew of that hadn't been raided. Aside from a few straggling drunks nipped on the streets near the speakeasy (which the coppers had still been unable to find), none of her patrons had been arrested on her watch. She was pretty proud of that.

The Feds had been trying to raid her club for months now, but not only could they not find the club itself, but Jessie's clever "fresh catch of the day" system of never being open on the same days, or at the same time any night, had paid off. This week, the joint was running on Monday, Thursday, and Saturday.

Those who wanted to know when the speakeasy would be open for business could come in, ask if the cod was fresh that day, and if it was a day when the speakeasy would be open, Jessie answered yes. If not, she'd answer no.

She did, of course, have customers who really wanted to buy the cod and had no idea that their asking after it might mean something else. But Jessie relied on her instincts and the penny in the bowl, to tell her if the person was after fish or a good time. For instance, Jessie had been fairly sure the harried mother with the two children clinging to her skirts had only been after something for supper. Though she had looked like she could have used a night on the town.

Jessie laughed silently, hoping she'd given the woman what she'd really wanted. But she hadn't dropped a penny in the bowl. That extra "payment" went a long way to weeding out whom to give the information to. No penny, no tip about The Red Phoenix.

Jessie tidied up the counter and then grabbed a broom, trying to stifle a yawn. Between running the shop by day and the speakeasy by night, she was past due on a few months worth of sleep. But without the profits from the speakeasy, she'd never have been able to keep the butcher shop running after her father had died. That not only meant keeping the shop open, but it also meant she could keep Joe and his grandson Charlie on the payroll. Selling some illegal liquor was worth it to keep them employed and the shop that she'd practically grown up in, open.

The little bell over the shop door tinkled and Jessie looked up to greet her new customer. She froze, struck momentarily goofy at the sight of the man in her doorway. She'd heard the expression "tall, dark, and handsome" before but had never seen a man who embodied it so completely.

She leaned on her broom mid-sweep to look up at the man through her lashes.

His broad shoulders nearly filled the narrow doorway, his suit jacket fitting a little too tightly across his biceps. The suit itself was good quality but had obviously seen better days. He took off his hat and the sunlight gleaming through the glass highlighted the slight shades of brown in his black hair. And those deep, chocolate brown eyes…well, if he wasn't just the bee's knees, she didn't know who was.

His full lips twitched into a smile and he cleared his throat. "Excuse me, are you open?"

"Oh!" Jessie said, startled back into awareness. Unfortunately, she'd forgotten about the broom and when she straightened, taking her weight off the handle, the bristles flung tiny bits of dust and debris straight into the man's face.

He gasped and stumbled back, brushing at his face.

"Oh, horsefeathers!" All the blood rushed to Jessie's cheeks and she slapped her hand over her mouth, mortified she'd let that slip. "I'm so sorry. Are you okay?"

The man blinked frantically, his eyes watering. "I think I've gotten a bit of something in my eye."

"Here." Jessie grabbed his arm and led him to a stool behind the counter. "Let me see."

The man straddled the stool and tilted his face up for Jessie to see. There wasn't much space behind the counter and in order for her to get close enough to look in his eye she had to stand between his legs. A position that made her cursed cheeks flame even hotter. Her father had always teased her about her penchant for blushing. Could read her emotions in her cheeks, he'd said. He'd affectionately called her "Rosie" from the first moment he'd seen her blush. He'd thought it was sweet. Jessie despised it.

She gave herself a mental slap and tried to pull it together. She'd probably blinded the poor man and all she could think about was how the muscled leg encased in his smart pinstriped suit was brushing against her thighs. It had been a while since she'd been this close to any man, let alone one handsome enough to make her sigh at the very sight of him.

She forced her attention to his eye, tilting his head farther up to the light. She pried his lid open and stared straight into his deep brown iris. The color reminded her of a bar of dark chocolate she'd once seen melted on the pavement outside… all silky smooth and utterly decadent.

"Do you see anything?" he asked.

Oh. Right. "Hang on. Yep, I think there is a little bit of something here…" She carefully swiped at the corner of his eye and removed the speck of dirt that clung there.

The man rubbed at his eye and smiled. "Thank you."

"I'm so sorry about that. I feel terrible. You must let me make it up to you. The chops are divine today. How about one on the house? It's the least I can do."

"That won't be necessary," he said, standing and coming around to the front of the counter. "I would like the chops. Two of them, actually. But I'm more than happy to pay for them."

"No, really, I insist," Jessie said, quickly wrapping up the best cuts she had available. "I won't take a dime."

"Well, then." He took the meat and his smile had the heat flaming in Jessie's face again. "If you won't let me pay for these, at least tell me your name."

"Jessica. Jessica Harlan."

"Pleased to meet you, Mrs. Harlan. I'm Tony Solomon."

"It's Miss Harlan. The shop belonged to my father before he died."

His brows rose faintly. "I'm sorry for his passing. You run it on your own now?"

Jessie nodded, more warily this time. She didn't like to impart too much personal information.

"Well, I've heard nothing but wonderful things. A friend recommended I come and I couldn't resist."

Jessie flushed with pleasure. She took great pride in the shop and was pleased that her customers were happy enough that they spread the word. "Thank you, Mr. Solomon."

"Please, call me Tony."

She smiled. "Well, Tony, is there anything else I can get for you?"

"Yes, actually," he said, leaning casually against the counter, his eyes quickly glancing about the shop before coming back to rest on her. "I was wondering if the trout was fresh tonight."

Jessie stiffened and looked Tony over again. He had the question mostly right, but he'd gotten the fish wrong. And no penny. Only one other person had ever come into her shop obviously seeking information without knowing about the penny. And that person had turned out to be working for the Feds. Which meant someone may have put Mr. Solomon up to asking. It was a cryin' shame. He was one tall drink of water, and then some, and it disappointed Jessie to no end to discover he might be nothing more than a cop, or worse, some stool pigeon who worked for them.

Then again, she had no proof he was up to something. Maybe he was just inept and had forgotten. Better to be safe than sorry, though.

She smiled brightly and walked to the fish counter. "Our fish is always fresh, brought in first thing every morning. I've got a lovely fillet here, if it's trout that you're wanting. Shall I wrap it up for you?"

Tony's brow furrowed in a slight frown but he quickly covered it with a smile. "That sounds great, thanks."

Jessie weighed it, wrapped it and handed it across to him. "That'll be thirty-two cents."

Tony looked a bit surprised. Maybe he'd assumed she wouldn't charge him for the fish since she hadn't charged him for the chops. But since the most likely reason he'd asked about the fish was to find out when The Red Phoenix would be running, and since his reasons for that, being that he didn't have the right pass code, were probably contrary to her business interests, well, he could pay for that big old fillet and be happy about it.

He slipped the money across to her with a smile that would have made a rabid dog roll over and purr like a kitten. "Your parents should have named you Rosie," he said with a wink, gently running a finger down her flaming cheek. She jerked back, her mouth dropping open. He grinned again. "It was very nice to meet you, doll. Keep the change."

"Likewise," she managed to say, her unease at his bungled attempt to get information fading in the light of his unmitigated cheekiness and intoxicating smile.

She watched him walk out the door, leaning over the counter until she could no longer see him through the window. Staring at him was definitely better than a stick in the eye, but then her ex had been a looker too and all that had gotten her was brokenhearted and betrayed. No, if it was one thing her time with Mario had taught her, it was that the wrapping didn't always match the package. She would never be so foolish again. Still, the handsome Mr. Solomon was up to something. So…she'd keep an eye on him, just in case. A dirty job, to be sure, but someone had to do it.

• • •

Tony left the butcher shop, irritation speeding his steps. Jameson waited impatiently for him in a small alleyway around the corner.

"Well, what did you find out?"

Tony tossed the wrapped fillet at him. "I found out that a fillet of trout will cost you thirty-two cents."

Jameson tossed the fish to the ground. "Then you must have asked wrong."

"I said exactly what you told me to say. It's not my fault your information was incorrect."

Jameson scowled and Tony turned to leave, his patience with his old colleague at an end.

"Solomon, wait. I might have another job for you."

"I did what you asked me to, Jameson, and only as a professional courtesy. A one-time deal. We're done here."

He spun on his heel and rounded the corner. Jameson

followed.

"Mr. Solomon!" Miss Harlan called out, hurrying toward him with his hat in her hand. Tony pulled up short and Jameson ducked back around the building. Jessica's eyes flicked to the corner but came back to rest on him with no suspicion in her gaze as far as he could discern.

"Miss Harlan, what can I do for you?" he asked, taking her elbow and leading her away from the alleyway.

"You left your hat in my shop," she said, holding it out for him.

"Ah, thank you." He took it from her and placed it back on his head. "That was kind of you."

She shrugged. "It will do more good on your head than on my countertop."

He chuckled. They'd reached her shop door and he took her hand, kissing the back. "It was a pleasure to see you again, Miss Harlan."

"Thank you, Mr. Solomon. Have a pleasant afternoon."

He watched her disappear back into her shop and resisted the urge to follow her. If Jameson was interested in her, she was nothing but trouble. He should walk away and put her from his mind. But then, he'd never been able to resist trouble. He glanced back to see Jameson leaning against the building by the alleyway, watching him with a calculating smile. A hard knot of unease settled in Tony's gut.

Jameson tipped his hat and disappeared back around the corner.

Chapter Two

When the bell over the shop tinkled just before closing time, Jessie looked up, half hoping the mouth-watering Mr. Solomon had decided to come back into her shop. Though she wasn't sure what she'd do if it *was* him. The man twisted her into knots and she didn't even know him. And she was pretty sure he'd been having a nice little chat with her best pal Jameson in a not-at-all suspicious alleyway. Which meant Jameson *had* put him up to asking about the fish…which annoyed her to no end.

She needn't have worried though. Instead of the handsome but confusing Mr. Solomon entering, it was the man who aggravated her much more.

"Agent Jameson. What I can I do for you this evening?"

"Ah now, Jessica. You know you can call me Earl."

"I know."

Jameson squinted, a little taken aback, but pushed on. "We didn't get to chat last time I stopped by."

"Not to sound rude, but why *do* you keep stopping in? I'm just a butcher, trying to run my business. I have no idea why I warrant constant visits by a prohibition agent."

"Maybe we just want to make sure butchering is all you are up to. After all, with your past associations…"

Jessie stiffened. Mario had ruined her life in more ways than one. She hadn't known who he was when she'd met him. Hadn't known he was part of Willie the Weasel's organization. And even though she was no longer with him, she was now considered *tainted*. Guilty by association. The unfairness of it nearly choked her, but she took a deep, focused breath and forced some politeness to the surface. Aggravating the little twit wouldn't make her life any easier, fun as it might be.

"As you said, Agent Jameson, those associations are in the *past*. I keep to myself now. I just want to run my business in peace."

"And how *is* business going? That's a nice new sign you've got above your window out there. Must have cost a pretty penny."

Jessie kept the smile on her face despite his insinuation. "Business is great. I've got the best meat in town and my customers know it."

"Well, that's real good to hear. I was afraid things might have slowed down for you. I haven't noticed too many customers coming in lately. The crowd when I stopped by the other day seems to be the exception now, rather than a regular occurrence."

Her eyes narrowed and she breathed deeply before answering. "Things are going just fine. And a friend of mine did the sign for me. Gave me a great price on it. Would you like something? Pig's ear? Beef tongue? I've got some nice chicken livers back here. I promise you won't find better anywhere."

"No thanks," he said, wrinkling his nose and giving her a smile that didn't reach his eyes. "You sure that's all you're selling?"

"What are you implying, Agent Jameson?"

He shrugged and leaned against the counter. "A few days ago, the local coppers brought in a man who was trying to sell a case of hooch that was an awful lot like the stuff your daddy used to make. Any idea how he got ahold of that?"

Jessie leaned over the counter, right in Jameson's face. "And how would you know his gin?"

"I ran it by a few of the other agents."

Jessie snorted. "The only reason they'd know is because they used to be some of my father's best customers."

"Be that as it may..."

She backed up a little and put her hands on her hips. "If it is from my father's stash then that man probably stole it. I had a break-in a few weeks ago and a couple cases went missing."

"Did you report the theft?"

"It's not illegal to own liquor, Agent Jameson. Just to sell it. But you and I both know that had I marched in to the police station to report the theft of a case of bathtub gin, I'd have been locked up faster than some flimflam man."

She grabbed a rag and continued wiping the counter she'd been cleaning when he'd come in. "I doubt many of the good officers would believe that I inherited a whole cellar full of the stuff."

Jameson smiled. "Well, you've probably got a point there. But if you don't want any trouble, why don't you just get rid of what you've got left? Remove the temptation, so to speak. From people who'd want to steal it, or sell it."

"I'm saving it for a rainy day," she said with a smile. Jameson didn't return it.

"That gin is all I've got left of my father. And someday when this silly Prohibition stuff is over with, I might be able to do something useful with the stock I've got. Until then, I'm sitting on it nice and tight."

Jameson studied her for a minute and then finally nodded.

"I'll let it go, for now. But if you are caught selling it…I won't be able to protect you from the consequences."

Jessie looked him right in the eye. "I give you my word that I'm not selling liquor, of any sort, out of my store."

He nodded again. "Well then. You have a good night, Jessica."

"Good night, Agent Jameson."

Jessie waited until he'd exited the shop, then followed behind him and locked the door, flipping her sign to Closed. She sighed with relief and finished tidying up for the night. She hadn't lied to Jameson. She wasn't selling any liquor out of the store. *Under* the store was a different matter, altogether.

She'd taken as many precautions as she could to keep her secrets. And they'd paid off. The Feds had never been able to connect The Red Phoenix directly to her. A situation helped by the fact that while the speakeasy was technically located beneath her shop, the public entrance was not.

Jessie had lucked out when she'd stumbled upon the network of old tunnels under her father's shop. While moving some stock in their cellar one night, she'd found a trapdoor. She'd taken the first opportunity to explore it. The narrow steps led to a tunnel that opened into a network of tunnels and a series of chambers. They must have been part of an old building that had been where her father's shop now stood.

Jessie had been immediately enchanted. The old stone was beautiful, with arched doorways and odd nooks and crannies cropping up now and then. Several other tunnels led off the rooms. Two had been bricked off. But one led to the street above, opening into a wide alleyway a block away from the butcher shop and a few others led to various alleyways in the neighborhood.

It was the perfect setup. The main room was large enough for a decent sized club, and the stone walls and the fact that it was underground, created enough of a sound barrier that nothing could be heard on the streets above. A few smaller chambers were used for storage and an office. The tunnel that led to the cellar in her shop was located in her office and she was the only one who knew of its existence.

The Feds could sit and watch her butcher shop all night long if they chose. And they had, a few times. They'd never see anything untoward occurring on the premises. Her speakeasy clientele would never step foot inside, except perhaps to buy meat…and for a penny, discover when The Red Phoenix would be open for business. Her private entrance to the club also meant that she could come and go as she pleased without anyone seeing her. The fact that her apartment was located above the shop meant no one questioned if they didn't see her leave. All of which allowed her to keep the identity of the Phoenix a secret.

When her father died, she'd tried to keep the butcher shop running, but she had lost a lot of clientele and she needed money to keep things going. Selling off a few cases of her father's gin had brought in some funds, but it had been too dangerous to sell in such quantities. And it had limited her source of income.

With the presence of the tunnels, opening a speakeasy had been the natural decision to make. After all, what else could a girl do with a secret underground paradise and a storeroom full of liquor? The speakeasy brought in more than enough to keep the shop running. She didn't have to even keep the shop open any longer. But closing it would spark too many questions and cost her the system of alerting speakeasy customers. Besides, it had been her father's shop. She'd never get rid of it.

But it was nice not having to rely on its income to keep bread on the table. Jameson was right, though. Her clientele had dropped lately, and not just in the shop. She'd noticed fewer patrons in the club the last few weeks. She'd heard of another speakeasy nearby that was under new management and doing quite well for itself.

Which made her wary, and curious, about who was poaching on her territory.

Chapter Three

Tony sat at his desk, shuffling through a stack of the most tedious paperwork he'd ever had the displeasure of filling out. And that was saying something. He'd filled out his share of tiresome reports when he was a cop. But they, at least, had been real cases. This one...Tony sighed. Another cheating husband and another wife who already knew, but wanted Tony to prove it. It sickened him.

He'd been on the fast track to becoming a federal agent and he'd been one of the youngest and most respected detectives on the police force. He was everything the Bureau of Investigation looked for in a new recruit. Until it had all blown up in his face.

A gust of wind blew the stack of papers off Tony's desk and he swore while he gathered them up. He swore even louder when he saw the reason for the breeze.

"What the hell are you doing here?" he asked the man who stood in his doorway.

"Now, that's no way to greet an old friend, is it?"

"You're no friend of mine, Jameson."

Jameson scowled and pulled out the seat on the opposite side of Tony's desk.

"Go ahead, have a seat," Tony said, scowling and slumping back into his own chair.

He glared at Jameson. Other than the run-in in front of the butcher dame's shop, they hadn't seen each other in almost two years, and Tony had no desire to see the man now.

"So, what do you want?"

"Always direct, aren't you?"

Tony shrugged. "No point in lollygagging. Spill it."

"I've got a job for you."

"I've got enough jobs," Tony said, leaning back in his chair and crossing his arms.

"Not one like this."

Tony cocked an eyebrow. "And why is that?"

"This one'll pay three times what any of those mediocre jobs are paying."

"Sure, I'll just have to sell my soul to do it. If it's something *you* don't want to dirty your hands with, what makes you think I'd want to do it?"

Jameson arched his own brow and Tony tried to rein in the anger that threatened to choke him. Once upon a time, Jameson had been a mentor, of sorts, but he'd been a weasely little snot then...and he still was. The difference was, Tony didn't have to put up with him anymore. "Get the hell out of my office, Jameson."

"This isn't really a choice, Solomon."

Tony's eyes narrowed. He had a feeling it'd be like that. Jameson wouldn't have come on his own accord. And if his bosses wanted Tony to do a job, it had to be because their own agents were too incompetent to do it.

That had been one of the reasons Tony had been interested in becoming an agent himself—he knew he'd be better at the job than any of the agents he'd come across. Jameson, himself a former detective who'd made the transition to the Bureau, had been assigned to make sure Tony was "Bureau" material. He had been, too. Until he'd gotten a little too cocky and a stupid mistake on a routine job had cost a good cop his life. Tony had been "allowed" to retire early. Any dreams of joining the Bureau had died along with his career.

"When did you decide to transfer to the Bureau of Prohibition?" Tony asked, stalling for a little time while his mind furiously spun.

Jameson's eyes narrowed. "A year ago. So, what's it going to be, Solomon? It's a good offer and you know it. You won't get another one like this if you pass this up. I know you tried to get back into law enforcement when you came back to town. And I know that none of the agencies would touch you. Not even the local police department of that podunk town you crawled out of when you sobered up. You didn't start this P.I. firm because you wanted to. You didn't have a choice. Well, now I'm offering you one. Don't throw this away."

Tony focused his attention out the window until he could control the urge to sock Jameson in his ugly mug. It was one thing to hate his job. It was another to have someone like Jameson point out how worthless it was. He'd like nothing more than to throw the man out of his office on his butt-kissing ass, but with Tony already on shaky ground with law enforcement agencies, he couldn't really afford to get on their wrong side. Worse than he was, anyway, not if he ever wanted to get out of this stinking office and salvage his career.

"What is it exactly that you are *requesting* I do?"

"There's a certain someone we need a little more information on."

Tony's eyes narrowed further, and he hated that he was a little intrigued. "And who is this certain someone?"

Jameson smiled. "Our little friend at the butcher shop. We need you to get a bit more...*cozy* with her. She's not really your type, but then," he looked around the office, "maybe you're ready for a change of pace, eh?"

The mention of the intriguing Miss Harlan made Tony's hand clench in an urge to slug Jameson.

"Just spill it and get the hell out of my office, Jameson. I already did your little favor and asked about the fish. What exactly is going on? She looked at me like I was crazy. And then stuck me with a fillet of trout, which I hate, and I had to *pay* for it."

"The fish is code, we believe, for when The Red Phoenix will be open. We thought we had the right phrasing nailed down. Apparently not."

"You honestly think that dame is involved with some speakeasy?"

Jameson dropped a file on Tony's desk and leaned back in his chair while Tony flipped it open with a knot in his stomach. He didn't know why he cared. She had seemed nice, though. Different. A female butcher? Making her way in the world alone? He admired her. And the way her cheeks had flushed every time he'd looked at her made him want to explore every inch of her deliciously rosy skin.

Jessie's picture stared up at him from the file. Her face was in profile, her thick hair blowing in the wind, though the black and white photo didn't do justice to its actual rich chestnut color. She was speaking to a gentleman whose face was obscured by the corner of a building. She obviously wasn't aware she'd been photographed. They'd had her under surveillance.

More pictures showed her with the same gentleman, though there was never a clear shot of his face. Tony's gut knotted at how obviously familiar the man was to Jessie. One picture showed him with his arm draped around her shoulder; another, opening a car door for her outside a restaurant. Another was shadowy, blurry, obviously taken through the shop window, but it looked like the man and Jessie were wrapped in an embrace, passionately kissing.

Tony tossed the pictures back on the desk, gritting his teeth against the rush of disappointment and anger the pictures dredged up. The file contained only a few other papers with almost no information. Her name—Jessica Harlan. Her age— twenty-five. Her address—an apartment above the butcher shop.

Tony arched an eyebrow. "Doesn't seem like much here. What makes you think this dame is involved in anything illegal?"

Jameson tapped his finger on the pictures. "That man."

Tony bit his tongue against responding to Jameson's condescending tone and looked more carefully at the pictures. He brought the clearest photo up to his face.

"You can't see him clearly enough to make him out. Who is he?"

"We think he's Mario Russo."

"Willie the Weasel's Mario Russo?"

"Live and in person," Jameson said, leaning back and folding his hands across his chest. "Or so we believe. Hard to tell from the pictures, but the scuttlebutt at the time was that it was none other than Russo. Which means our little Miss Harlan spent several months running around town with one of the highest ranking members of Willie's organization. Not looking so innocent now, is she?"

Tony's swallowed, his stomach dropping a notch or two. "And now?"

"They had some sort of falling out—"

"Maybe she figured out who he was and cut ties."

Jameson's eyebrow rose at the interruption. "Maybe. But word on the street is that she found herself a bigger fish."

Tony didn't want to know who that might be. The thought of her being some gangster's moll ruined the shiny picture he'd had of her in his head. He glanced back at the thin file. "You don't seem to have any information on any other man. What makes you think she's involved with anyone? Especially someone who runs in Russo's circles?"

Jameson shrugged. "Miss Harlan's shop floundered after her father died. And then suddenly it started flourishing again. Though there hasn't been a noticeable influx of new customers. And her father was famous around these parts for his gin. Before Prohibition, of course. Made the stuff his whole life. She doesn't keep it in her shop that we can tell, so where did it all go? She apparently dug up enough clams from somewhere to save her shop, so where did the money come from?"

"You must have some idea."

"We do."

Jameson tossed another file onto the desk, one even thinner than Miss Harlan's, if that were possible. "The Phoenix? Really?"

Jameson shrugged again. "That's what he's known by. Owns a speakeasy called The Red Phoenix."

Tony flipped the single sheet in the file over. "That's all you know about him? His name and the name of his club? How do you even know he exists? Or that he's involved with Miss Harlan?"

"We have our sources."

Tony snorted and tossed the file down on his desk. "Then why can't these sources get the information you need? Why come to me?"

"She's cagey." He shrugged. "But a skirt's a skirt. And you've always been able to attract the dames with that good-looking mug of yours. I'm sure it'd be no problem for a man like you to charm some information out of her. Might be easier to get what we need if she's carrying a torch for you. Catch more flies with honey and all that."

Jameson looked out the window and Tony smiled. Jameson could squawk all day about charm and good looks, but Tony knew why they'd come to him. Because when it came to undercover work, he was the best. It must gall Jameson to have to admit it, though. Tony sat there and watched him squirm, enjoying the jackass being on the other end of their little game for a change.

Finally, he relented. "So what exactly do you want me to do?"

"We want you to find the Phoenix and bring him in. His speakeasy has become the hottest spot in town. Only we've never been able to pinch anyone on a raid. Every time we think we've got some credible information about where the damn place is, all we find are empty storerooms."

"You don't know where the joint is? You've never caught anyone?"

Jameson grimaced. "A few tanked stragglers wandering around on the street, but a thorough search of the buildings they are found near has never turned anything up. Nothing to indicate a speakeasy has ever been in the area. The man is more clever than most. We never know when the place is up and running and wouldn't know where to look even if we did. And like I said, the few times we've gotten reliable information, we didn't find anything."

"And how does this dame factor in to all this?"

"She's his girl. And if you want to know when the club is open, you need to go to her shop to find out."

The knot in Tony's gut hardened and he swallowed. "Then just pick her up. Question her."

Jameson pinned him with an exasperated look. "We already have. She won't talk."

"And you can't make her?" Tony couldn't keep the smugness out of his voice and Jameson's face darkened.

"We've had men tailing her for months. She's careful.

And until now we didn't know the pass phrase to get the information on the club."

"No offense, but since it didn't work, I'd say you still don't know it."

Jameson glowered at him.

"Why not just send another agent in? I'm sure you've got enough men hanging around doing nothing."

Jameson smiled, though there was nothing friendly about it. "We want a little more than just finding out the nights the club is open."

Tony frowned. He didn't like where this was going.

"We also need to know particulars about the club. Where is it? How are people getting out? Who's the supplier? Where are the stores of liquor? Especially where the liquor is. For Miss Harlan's own protection, of course."

"What do you mean?"

"As far as we can tell, the Phoenix isn't bootlegging across any of the supply chains we've come across. He could be a rumrunner, transporting the stuff by ship, across the lakes, but the more likely option is that the Phoenix is either using Miss Harlan's father's stock, or she's making the stuff herself to supply him. But if she's buying it from someone else to keep his club stocked, it's not from Willie the Weasel. Because he's taken an unhealthy interest in her."

Both Tony's eyebrows shot up at that. If Willie was interested, the club must be doing quite well, indeed.

"Wouldn't her involvement with Russo already have brought her to Willie's attention?"

"Not to this extent. We had no interest in her ourselves until right around the time she split with Russo. That's when word started spreading about the Phoenix and his new speakeasy. And this dame's involvement. Not long after that, Russo is out of the picture and The Red Phoenix is the hottest ticket in town."

"Even so, why does Willie care if one little speakeasy does well? Surely it's not making that big of a dent in his profits."

Jameson shrugged again. "Enough that he's taken notice. Apparently, The Red Phoenix is a jumping joint and if the Phoenix is selling Miss Harlan's gin, then he's not buying Willie's. That's rubbing Willie the wrong way."

"He's got men watching her, too?"

Jameson nodded and Tony whistled. "So what are the specifics? You want the club, the booze, and the Phoenix?"

Jameson nodded.

"She's not going to give any of that up easily."

"Of course not," Jameson said, leaning over the table. "Which is why we wanted you for the job."

Anger burned its way through Tony's gut. It wasn't his skills as a P.I. that the agency wanted. It was his pretty face.

"You want me to romance it out of her."

Jameson smiled. "If necessary. Should be easy enough for you. And much more fun than any of the jobs you've been running lately. She's not so bad to look at."

The thought of what they wanted him to do made Tony sick. "She's a lady, not some floozy."

"And you know that from talking to her for all of two minutes?"

Tony didn't trust himself to answer. His anger on her behalf was irrational and he couldn't explain where it was coming from. The evidence, circumstantial though it was, was damning enough that he could understand why the Feds were interested. But he'd be willing to bet his hat that Jessica Harlan wasn't what they thought.

"She's not a lady. She's the whore of a criminal, and not for the first time. Even if she's not directly involved with his activities, she's far enough in. She's guilty by association and I'm sure by a lot more. It's your job to find out how far in she is."

Tony shook his head. "No. I'm not using some poor girl just because you can't do your job."

"Oh, grow up, Solomon. She's neck deep in this and you know it. You want to know where the speakeasy is, you go to her. The place is probably selling her father's booze. She's using profits from the club to keep her shop running. She's just as much a criminal as the Phoenix is. Her pretty face doesn't change that fact."

Tony sat back, still fuming. Jameson actually made a compelling argument, though he hated to admit it. Still…

"Besides, here's your incentive."

Jameson tossed an envelope on his desk and Tony glanced down at it.

"Open it."

Tony didn't want to comply, but his curiosity, and his empty bank account, got the better of him. The amount on the check made his blood run cold. And he hated himself for it. He wanted that money. Needed it. It would keep his rent paid for the next year, at least. More importantly, he could finally do right by his mother, find her a nice place uptown, and get her out of the dump she was in.

"You must want this man bad."

"We need to make an example of him."

"Why him?"

"So far, he's not as dangerous as Capone or Willie. He's not claiming any dead bodies, yet, so taking him down should be easier. His entire organization, as far as we can tell, is her," he said, pointing to the file that still lay open on Tony's desk. "It won't be as flashy as one of the bigger fish, but it'll make a bigger impact. This man is one of their own. He's not some mysterious mobster running things from his private fortress."

"That you know of."

Jameson nodded. "That we know of. For all we know, he *is* Capone. We know he isn't in Willie's organization, because

Willie's got his own men watching her. But even Capone and Willie haven't been immune. Their speakeasies have been raided. Their operations interrupted. Not the Phoenix. We want him. And with you, we might be able to get him."

Tony took a deep breath. He didn't like this job. He had a bad feeling about it, and he'd learned to trust those feelings. And he really didn't want to get involved with Jameson again.

Though…this could be his chance. If he pulled this off, if he could bring in the Phoenix, he could vindicate himself and prove that he was better than the mistake he'd made. Maybe he'd even be allowed back on the force. Start working his way back up the ladder into the Bureau of Investigation. At the very least, it would do wonders for his P.I. business. A picture of him in the paper, an article showcasing how he'd brought down the notorious Phoenix. He'd have more jobs than he knew what to do with.

"I'm afraid I can't give you time to think about this. We need an answer now."

"And when would this job start?"

"Immediately."

"Details?"

Jameson smiled, probably figuring he had him where he wanted him. Tony kept his grimace to himself. Let the man think whatever he wanted.

"We recently shut down a speakeasy not far from where Miss Harlan's shop is located. We'll set you up as the owner—with the same employees, and start spreading word around town that your joint is the hot new one to frequent."

Tony's eyes widened. "You're going to run your own speakeasy in order to catch this guy? Shaving the legal line a little thin there, aren't you?"

"We've gotten permission from the higher ups. For a short time."

"They must really be desperate to get this guy."

"Aside from the fact that he's breaking half a dozen or so laws, he's Willie's new favorite hobby. That means we could have a full-scale territory war on our hands. I don't care if a bunch of rumrunners kill themselves. Saves me the trouble of hauling them in. But they could potentially take out a lot of innocent people and terrorize the entire city in the process. The last thing we want is a massacre on our hands or widespread panic if these gangsters start shooting it out in the streets. If we have to sell some very watered-down booze to prevent that from happening, well, it's a necessary evil. However, we do have a ticking clock on this."

Tony's stomach sank. "And exactly how fast is it ticking?"

"You've got a month."

Tony laughed out loud. "A month. To bring this dame in, get her to trust me enough to spill her guts about her boyfriend, find him and his rumrunning operation, and gather enough evidence to shut the place down and lock him up for good."

Jameson crossed his arms over his chest and smiled. "That's right. The speakeasy we seized was only down for a few nights. The patrons think it was just a normal raid and business is back to usual. We've quietly spread the word that it's under new management, and the new owner, you, will be making an appearance shortly. So all you need to do is get the dame in line."

Tony leaned back in his chair and stretched his arms, locking his fingers behind his head. "You're out of your mind."

"What's the matter, Tony? Don't think you can do it? What happened to that first class reputation of yours? Wasn't too long ago all you had to do was look at a lady to have her offering up every secret she ever had on a silver platter. Losing your touch?"

Tony dropped his arms, his body going tense again. "This isn't some regular dame. According to you, she's the girl of one of the best rumrunners in the city. I'm sure she's wise to any games cops wanna play."

"Well, then," Jameson said, standing up and straightening his jacket. "I guess you'll just have to come up with some new games. Of course, if The Corkscrew is successful enough, starts hurting his bottom line, that alone might draw the Phoenix out. If not…"

"If I can't draw him out for poaching his business, you want me to draw him out by poaching his dame."

Tony scowled and Jameson lost the smile. "I can try and buy you some more time. But it won't be much."

Tony nodded. "Anything you can get would be helpful."

Jameson opened the door. "I'll expect bi-weekly reports from you. And if you get anything of importance, come to me immediately."

Tony frowned, hating to be back under Jameson's command. But he saw the check sitting on the desk and nodded.

He felt like he was selling his soul to the devil, but if it would get his career back on track, and set his mother up for whatever time she had left, then the devil had himself a new partner.

Chapter Four

Jessie looked out over the crowded club with a sense of satisfaction and pride. There was no electricity in the tunnels, and she liked it that way. The flickering candles and gas lamps she used created an air of sensuous mystery while helping to keep everyone safe from the Feds at the same time.

The Red Phoenix had never actually been raided, but it had come close a time or two. Close enough that Jessie had cleared the place out, just to be safe. Instead of clanging alarms or flashing lights, the lamps at The Red Phoenix were quickly extinguished until only the large mining lantern set on a pole near the entrance and the candles on the tables were left. Patrons were encouraged to take the candles with them to help light the way while one of the band members would grab the lantern and lead them out through the tunnels.

Those who quit flapping their lips and followed quickly and quietly were led to safety, through the tunnels and out one of the many exits. Those who panicked and tried to flee back through the entrance were the ones who got pinched. After the first time this happened, word had spread that if you wanted to get out, you shut up and followed the big light.

The rest of the band members and crew would stash the "bar"—old doors set on casks of gin—back against the wall, and the remaining casks that served as tables were left where they sat strewn haphazardly about the room. If the Feds arrived, they'd find nothing but an empty storage room. One that, thanks to the winding tunnels, they had no idea sat just below Jessie's shop.

The stage where the band played had proved the only problem until Joe had come up with the ingenious solution of putting it on rolling castors that could be locked into place when they played. The stage was positioned near the entrance to one of the bricked-up tunnels that was closed off with a metal gate. The lock on the gate had been easy enough to pick and during business hours it was left open. Afterward, or during a raid, the entire stage could be shoved into the tunnel, covered with old tarps, and locked back up behind the metal gate, appearing, for all the world, like another heap of forgotten junk.

It was a good setup. Primitive but utterly suitable for those looking for a clandestine drink. Besides, the medieval surroundings gave The Red Phoenix a certain nostalgic romance that people seemed to love. And the sultry tones coming from Jessie's top-billed songstress lent the speakeasy a hearty helping of sex appeal. The makeshift tables were full of laughing patrons perched on overturned buckets and reinforced boxes, drinking her father's best home gin, and since she never watered down what she served and she didn't have a drink limit, her club was very popular.

She'd be able to stay open longer if she rationed out the gin, but the business's longevity wasn't her goal. She wanted to make as much money as fast as she could so she could get out of the racket before either the Feds or Willie the Weasel got wise to her game. Both wanted to shut her down, but for entirely different reasons. She wasn't going to let either of them ruin what she'd worked so hard to build. Not until she could get out from under the ax hanging over her head.

Jessie's father had been a good man and had worked hard every day of his life, but business hadn't been going so great in the months before his death, and he'd had to take out a few loans from men he didn't realize were part of Willie the Weasel's crew. Willie wanted his money paid back in full, with interest, and the butcher shop just didn't bring in enough. With the speakeasy, she was well on her way to paying off the debt.

She'd even been able to start a little nest egg, something she'd heavily debated doing. Paying off Willie as soon as possible was something she absolutely needed to do. But getting that debt squared away would do her no good if she didn't have the funds necessary to keep the butcher shop up and running. In the end, she'd decided to bank on her future needs, even if it meant delaying getting Willie out of her life by a few months.

Besides, paying him off too quickly might make him more curious than he already was about The Red Phoenix and how well it was doing. He'd been somewhat lenient about her speakeasy rivaling his own joints because he was getting a nice cut of the action. Too much dough rolling in might hurt her more than help.

Things were going well. An end was finally in sight. She just needed a little more time.

Time she wasn't sure she had, thanks to her sadistic ex. Yes, she'd owed Willie money before ever meeting Mario, but he was the one who'd brought The Red Phoenix, and her association with it, to Willie's attention. And Willie had noticed that the club was supplied with liquor that didn't come from him. His growing interest in the matter was a constant gnawing fear Jessie couldn't shake. *Thank you, Mario*, she thought snidely.

"Hey, boss. Pour me one, will you?"

Jessie frowned at Maude, tonight's entertainment and her best friend, but poured her a drink.

"Oh don't be such a flat tire," Maude said. "I need my giggle water. Singin's hard work."

"This stuff'll ruin your voice if you keep downing it like that."

"Naw. It'll keep it nice and raspy, just the way the boys like it." She winked at Jessie, who couldn't help but smile at the vivacious blonde.

Maude had curves in all the right places and a voice that left men, and a few women, quivering in their seats. Jessie thanked her lucky stars for the day that Maude had walked into her joint looking for work. They'd known each other as children, but it had been years since she'd seen her. Jessie had been on the hunt for a good voice and had been ready to take the stage herself until Maude had sauntered in. Jessie had been thrilled to see her old friend again and even more thrilled to offer her a job. Maude had been solid gold dynamite, and between her singing and Jessie's father's booze, The Red Phoenix stayed packed. And profitable.

"So, you hear about The Corkscrew?" Maude rolled her eyes. "Supposedly under new management after their last raid. Been pretty busy since then. I hear the mook who runs the place now is a real looker."

Jessie laughed. "Folks are probably going just to get a look at his pretty mug."

"Maybe. Wouldn't mind getting a gander at him myself. Hey Joe," she said, leaning across the bar to flag him down. "Butt me, will ya?"

Joe chuckled and handed her a ciggy, pushing a candle in her direction so she could light it. She turned back to Jessie, blowing out a ring of smoke. "If I were you, I'd drop in on him and see what all the fuss is about. The crowd is looking a little thin tonight."

Jessie looked back over the patrons. Maude was right. The place was still hopping, but normally at this time of night, it should be standing room only.

"Maybe I will. Wouldn't hurt to see what the competition is offering."

"And what we can do to make sure what we're offering is better," Maude said, stubbing out her cigarette and smoothing her hands over her voluptuous hips.

Jessie laughed. "No worries, Maudey, my dear, no one can offer what you've got going."

"Well, of course not."

Maude winked at Jessie and sauntered back to the stage.

• • •

Tony sat beside his mother's bed, watching her as she slept. He frowned, trying to push back the worry that clutched at his heart like a vise. She seemed frailer than last week. Tiny against the pillows, the hand that lay on the blankets looked wrinkled and tinged with gray. He leaned forward, his elbows on his knees, and took her hand in his own. The hand that had so often soothed him when he'd needed it as a boy. Or more often had wielded a wooden spoon, threatening his hide. He hadn't been the best behaved kid in the world.

The memories brought a small smile to his face. She was small, but she was fierce. She was all he had left in the world. His pa had died years ago and Tony was an only child. A surprise to his parents after twenty childless years. When she was gone, he'd be alone.

Her hand tightened on his and he looked up to find her watching him.

"Hi, Ma."

She gave his hand another squeeze and he was encouraged by the strength he still felt in it.

"I'm not gone yet, my boy. I've still got a few good years left in me, so stop looking at me like that."

Tony laughed and leaned forward to kiss her forehead. "Yes, ma'am."

"What are you doing here? You were just here to see me yesterday. Everything all right?"

Tony smiled and patted her hand. "Sure, Ma. Everything's aces."

"*Hmm*. What's going on?"

"Nothing. I just wanted to visit, that's all."

Her quizzical gaze pierced him straight through. His ma could see through anyone and anything. He laughed. "Never could pull anything over on you."

"No, you couldn't. Don't know why you still bother trying. Now tell me what's going on in that head of yours that has you coming up here in the middle of the week when you should be working."

Tony sighed and leaned forward a little more, placing his other hand over the top of hers. "Jameson stopped by my office yesterday."

His mother's eyebrows rose at that. "I'm guessing he didn't come in to offer you a job."

Tony shook his head. "Not full time, no. But they do want me to do something for them."

"And you don't want to do it?"

"I'm not sure." He let go of her hands, sat back, and rubbed at his face. "They offered me more than I make in a year doing P.I. work."

Mrs. Solomon's wrinkled eyes widened. "They must want you pretty bad."

"I don't think they have any other options. They want me to get some information about a man."

"That shouldn't be too hard for you."

"No," Tony said, frowning.

"But?"

"But…they want me to get close to this man's girl, get the information out of her."

Mrs. Solomon patted her son's hand. "And you don't feel right using a woman like that."

"If she's part of his organization, she's just as much of a criminal as he is and deserves to be locked up."

"But you don't think she is?"

"I don't know. I've only met her once. She's a bit cagey, could definitely be hiding something. She's been mixed up with some shady characters in the past. But, there's something about her…"

"Really?" Mrs. Solomon smiled faintly and Tony groaned.

"It's not like that."

She shrugged. "So you say."

"Ma," he warned, and she held up her hands.

"I'm not saying anything about anything." She reached over and took his hand again. "You are a good man. I've never known you to do anything you didn't feel was right."

Tony opened his mouth to argue but she stopped him. "Everyone makes mistakes, my boy. You need to let the past lie in the past. You've more than made up for what happened, more than you needed to. Accidents happen; you were no more responsible than anyone else."

"That's not the way the department or the Bureau saw it."

"Idiots. Every last one of them. You were the only one with any brains in that place. And the fact that they are coming to you now just proves it."

Tony smiled. She always had his back.

"You worry too much," she said, squeezing his hand. "You've got a good heart and a good head on your shoulders.

Trust in those."

Tony stood and gathered her to him, surprised as always at how small and light she felt in his arms. She wrapped her arms around his neck and patted his head, just like she'd done since he was a little boy.

"I love you, Ma."

She pulled back and held his face in her hands, then pulled him down to kiss his forehead. "Love you, too. Now," she said, patting his cheeks. "Go catch those criminals."

Tony smiled and left his mother with a lighter heart. She always helped him put things in perspective.

Chapter Five

Jessie hummed as she worked, the meaningless notes turning into a song after a few moments. She loved to sing, truth be told, though having an audience made her more nervous than she could stand. So she avoided doing it in front of people, except for the odd Sunday at church.

But now, when there was no one to hear her but the uncut beef hanging in the freezer, she could let her voice ring out. She belted out the lyrics to "It Had to Be You," picturing a pair of gorgeous brown eyes watching her as she sang.

"You have a beautiful voice."

Jessie screamed at the top of her lungs, jumping so hard her back slammed against the wall. She grabbed the nearest knife she could get her hands on, her other hand clutching her chest like some old biddy having an episode.

"Sorry," Tony said, chuckling and holding his hands up, "didn't mean to startle you."

She dragged in a few deep breaths, trying to calm the furious pounding of her heart. Here he was, conjured by her thoughts almost, popping up out of the blue. *What gives?*

"What are you doing here?"

"My apologies. I mean no harm," he said, looking down at her hand.

She glanced down, belatedly realizing she was still brandishing a knife at him. "Oh," she said, dropping it back on the counter. "Sorry."

"Entirely my fault. I didn't realize you hadn't heard me come in."

Jessie waved him off. It wasn't his fault she'd been too preoccupied to hear the bell. But with her heart still in her throat, she wasn't feeling generous enough to admit that.

"What can I do for you?" Jessie asked.

He tilted his head and studied her for a moment. Her eyes narrowed, not quite glaring at him, but enough to let him know she didn't appreciate being ogled.

"Do you sing, Miss Harlan?"

"Obviously, Mr. Solomon," she said dryly.

"No," he chuckled. "I mean do you sing professionally?"

"I am a butcher, Mr. Solomon. I sing for enjoyment, for myself. And occasionally in church if I'm feeling particularly adventurous."

He laughed again. "Please call me Tony. I think that is the first time I've heard the words *adventurous* and *church* mentioned in the same sentence."

Jessie shrugged, her mouth twitching into a smile despite herself. "I enjoy singing. I'm just not so good at doing it in front of an audience."

"*Hmm.*" Tony rubbed at his chin and studied her some more. "That's a shame."

"And why is that?"

"Well, after hearing what you are capable of, I'd hoped to convince you to come work for me."

"Work for you? Doing what?"

Tony glanced around and Jessie followed his gaze. They

were alone in the shop, but Tony leaned forward over the counter anyway.

"How do you feel about Prohibition, Miss Harlan?"

Jessie's eyes widened. Was this why he was here? To find out information on her? Well, she could play along for a bit, see what he was fishing for.

"To be honest, I'm not a fan of it."

He cocked an eyebrow and Jessie added, "But it is the law so…"

Implying that she followed the law wasn't the same as lying about it, right?

Tony did another quick glance around and leaned in a little farther. "Have you ever been to a speakeasy, Miss Harlan?"

Now Jessie's eyes widened. What was he getting at? "Have you, Mr. Solomon?"

"Call me Tony."

"Call me Jessie."

"Fine. Jessie. And to answer your question, though you don't seem willing to answer mine—Yes, I have."

Jessie smiled a little at his chiding tone. "Since you answered first, then yes, I have, as well."

"And would you consider working in a speakeasy? Singing. Because if you would, I have just the one in mind."

Realization dawned on her and Jessie sucked in a slow breath. He wanted her to work for him? "Do you own a speakeasy, Mr…Tony?"

The bell tinkled and Tony straightened up, moving down the counter a ways and pretended to peruse the meat selections under the glass. He glanced at her every now and then, but after a few minutes of a steady stream of customers, he put his hat on and headed for the door.

Jessie nearly called him back but stopped herself. Turned out not to be necessary. Tony tipped his hat and said, "Think about it. I'll be back tomorrow," before he walked out the door.

The woman she was waiting on gave her a knowing smile, waggling her eyebrows. "My, he certainly is handsome, isn't he?"

Jessie muttered something noncommittal and turned back to her meat.

How would the woman feel if she knew that Tony had just asked to her sing in his speakeasy?

More importantly, how did Jessie feel?

After a restless night thinking about it, she still wasn't sure. When he walked back into her shop the next morning, Jessie's traitorous heart leaped at the sight of his handsome face and the charming smile he bestowed on her sent a tingling warmth down to her toes. She pushed the feelings away the second they surfaced. Yes, he was handsome. But she knew nothing else about him except that he somehow knew Jameson. And that was not a mark in his favor.

The thoughts spinning around in her head were giving her a headache and she closed her eyes, flinching against the pain throbbing in her temples. The man was a mystery, plain and simple. One she'd like to get to the bottom of, for her own peace of mind, if nothing else.

She gave him a polite smile in return, trying her best to keep the rest of her roiling emotions from spilling over.

"Well. Mr. Solomon. Back so soon?"

"I thought I asked you to call me Tony," he said, his smile softening into something much more suitable for the bedroom.

Jessie bit her lip and turned her back, pretending to fiddle with some butcher paper until she was sure her face was composed.

"And yes, I just couldn't stay away. Have you made a decision?"

Jessie wiped her hands on a towel, taking a moment to word her response carefully. Tony seemed harmless, nice even. But the owner of a speakeasy large enough to need entertainment meant he wasn't running some little mom-and-pop operation. Which meant she'd need to watch her back around him.

"Not quite yet."

Tony rubbed his finger over his lips. "And what would it take to convince you?"

Jessie leaned against the counter, doing a little perusing of her own. "I don't know anything about you or what kind of joint you might be running."

"Fair enough. My place is called The Corkscrew."

Jessie's eyebrows raised.

"You've heard of it?"

She nodded. "I've heard it was under new management."

Tony gave her a little bow, his lips tweaking into a sexy half-smile that made Jessie want to toss her apron to the floor and run off with him right then and there. What on earth was wrong with her? She'd only gone goofy over a man once before and it had brought her nothing but a world of hurt. Now was no time to make the same mistakes all over again.

"I hear business has been going well for you."

"So far, yes," Tony said. "However, as I previously stated, we could use a little entertainment. I have a great band. We just need a dame with a set of pipes who can keep the place hopping. I've even got a stockpile of dresses you can wear."

"I'm not sure…I've never been there…"

"Well, that's easily remedied." He pulled out a card and slid it across the counter to her. "Be at that address tonight and I'll show you around."

Jessie stared at the card in her hand, blank aside from a one-line address. Her brow furrowed. She'd wanted to check out the competition. But she hadn't counted on the new owner of the place being so...appealing. Her unexpected attraction to him was throwing her for a loop.

She hadn't felt the slightest interest in any man since Mario, and Mr. Solomon was definitely the wrong man to start carrying a torch for. He was dangerous for her. Getting involved with him could put her out of business, put her in jail, or get her heart broken again. All scenarios she wanted to avoid at all costs. And the riot of nerves erupting in her stomach at the thought of singing in front of an audience couldn't be healthy. She certainly hadn't planned on performing at the joint.

"Come on," Tony urged, taking her hand. "What have you got to lose, eh?"

His thumb rubbed lazy circles over the back of her hand and Jessie heard herself responding before she'd consciously made a decision. "All right then. I'll see you tonight."

Tony gave her a dazzling smile that she returned before she could stop herself.

"Midnight," he said, bringing her hand up to his lips.

"Midnight," Jessie whispered, distracted by the warmth that was spreading from where his lips lingered on her skin clear up her arm and straight into her chest.

He released her, put his hat back on with a little nod. "Until tonight."

Jessie nodded back, her mind and body in too much turmoil to realize what she'd just agreed to until he'd already left the shop. When she finally snapped out of it, she groaned and sank down onto the stool behind the counter.

"What the hell did I just get myself into?" she muttered.

Well...she'd wanted to check him out. His club, that is. Looked like she was about to get up close and personal with the competition.

Chapter Six

"Have you lost your mind?" Maude said as Jessie grabbed her best dress out of her closet and laid it on the bed. She wanted the perfect outfit for tonight.

"Jessie! Are you even listening to me?"

Jessie sighed. "Yes, I'm listening. And no, I'm not crazy. It's the best way to find out what I'm up against. You were the one who told me I should check it out."

Maude put her hand on her hip, her expression clearly saying she didn't buy that excuse for a second. "Yes, check it out. Not dive right in and work for the competition! Doesn't he think you are the Phoenix's girl, like everyone else? What is the man thinking, asking you to work for him? And what's he going to think if you accept? You don't need to go playing private dick to get the score on this guy."

"I'm not going get the information I need as an outsider. I need to be an employee, one of them. Then maybe I can see what's really going on with him and Jameson, *and* see what's drawing the crowds. What Tony's got going for him that I don't."

Besides those dark bedroom eyes, tousled hair that looked like he'd just stepped out of bed, and a body that screamed for attention even through the well-fitting navy pinstriped suit he'd been wearing.

She had no doubt why women showed up in droves. She'd pay good money to sit and stare at the club's handsome owner. She'd done a good bit of staring when he had walked into her shop, and she needed to stop doing that. Tony seemed like the kind of man who was game for a little fun but Jessie wasn't anyone's floozy, despite what the Feds thought. She feared ignoring Tony wasn't going to be all that easy, though. She could still feel his firm grip on her hand, his fingers drawing circles on her skin while they had talked.

She shook her head and went back to getting ready. She couldn't afford any distractions. With Willie the Weasel breathing down her neck about her dad's debt and her siphoning off some of his bootlegging business, Tony's new joint stealing more customers every night, and the Feds always just around the corner, ready to catch her if she slipped up in any way, she needed to keep her head on her shoulders. And she couldn't do that if she was goofy over some man. Especially *this* man. He was her competition, for goodness' sakes. And that was the best case scenario. He could be in cahoots with the Feds. She needed to take him down, not take him to bed.

A warmth low in her belly at the mere thought of being in bed with Tony uncovered the lie in that little thought, but she ignored it. She'd done well enough without a man since Mario had used her and left her in a million little pieces. She'd do just fine for a little longer.

She slung her dress over her shoulder and headed for the door, ignoring Maude's dire muttered warnings. It was show time.

• • •

Tony's bored gaze swept over his club one more time, but nothing even remotely interesting had occurred since the last time he'd checked the crowd. Business was booming, with more and more people filtering in every night. The owners of the rival speakeasies were starting to take notice, which was a good thing. Hopefully soon, he'd be able to ferret out *someone* who could give him a little information on what he was truly after. The identity of the Phoenix.

This nightclub owner gig wasn't nearly as fun as he'd thought it would be, especially since he still hadn't gotten any information he could use. Jameson and his bosses would get restless soon if he didn't start producing something good for them and he'd be back to cooling his heels in his jalopy of a P.I. office instead of paintin' the town as the manager of the hottest joint around.

Tony knocked back the finger of whiskey in his glass and slid the empty along the bar to his bartender George, who neatly scooped it up and stashed it in the dirty bin. Tony's attention wandered to the sole entrance to the club, the smooth liquor running down his throat suddenly catching at the sight that met his eyes.

He coughed and blinked his watering eyes a few times. Jessie's smooth brown hair was sleeked back in a sequined headband and fell in rippling waves to her shoulders. The red silk dress she wore hugged every one of her delectable curves, the fringe attached to the material swinging tantalizingly with every move she made. Her fingers played with a long strand of knotted pearls that hung from her slender neck. She glanced around the club, her bright red-painted lips pursed.

Tony was on his way to her before he'd decided to move. She glanced up, her mouth a little *O* of surprise when he stopped in front of her.

"Good evening," he said, taking her gloved hand and pressing a kiss to it. "You look absolutely mouthwatering tonight, Miss Harlan."

"Thank you," she said, forcing the words out as though she didn't have enough air in her lungs to speak properly.

"I'm glad you decided to come. Shall I show you to a table?"

Her eyes met his and he fought the urge to suck in a breath. Those startlingly blue eyes of hers raked over him from crown to toe. The contrast with her deep brown hair rocked him and it took him a moment to realize she hadn't answered him yet.

He cocked an eyebrow at her. She blinked, her lips twitching into a chagrined smile. Hmm, perhaps she'd found his appearance to her liking as well. One could hope. His brand new suit felt like butter against his skin. Smooth and fitted to perfection. The knowledge that she was looking and liking what she saw sparked a smoldering heat low in his belly.

"That would be lovely, thank you."

Tony led her to one of his best tables, right up front near the stage. He helped her into a chair but kept hold of her hand even after she'd been seated. She glanced up at him, a perfectly groomed eyebrow raising. He took the seat next to her.

"So, what do you think of my place?"

Jessie looked around, lingering on every corner of the club as if she were truly appraising it and not just humoring him. "It's nice."

"Just nice?"

"Well, I'm partial to The Red Phoenix."

"Yet, tonight you are here."

She shrugged. "You invited me and I wanted to see what all the hullabaloo was about."

"And does it live up to your expectations?"

Her gaze explored him again and his body responded to her perusal as though it were her hands running over him and not her eyes. He wasn't used to being on the receiving end of one of those looks. He liked it. Very much. At least coming from her.

"More than."

"I'm glad to hear it."

She stared at him a moment and then looked away. He swore he detected one of her telltale blushes beneath her rouge. Good. Perhaps she was just as affected as he was. He still held her hand, and she'd made no move to pull it from his grasp. His fingers tightened slightly and she looked back at him.

"So, Jessie. What can I get for you this evening? Aside from a job, which I've yet to hear an answer about," he said, teasingly. "I'm curious, with that voice you've got, why don't you sing at The Red Phoenix, since you say you are a regular there?"

"They've got Maude Fairfax. They don't need me."

"If you're still not sure, why don't we give you a little trial? See how you like it?"

"A trial?"

"Sure. Hell, even if you couldn't sing—and I know you can—my patrons would probably pay extra just to sit there and look at you for an hour a night."

Jessie's cheeks flushed the same red as her dress. It was utterly adorable and it surprised Tony how much he wanted to pull her back to his office to see if she was blushing everywhere.

Jessie nodded. "All right. Do you have an office or something? I can sing for you."

Tony shook his head and stood, drawing her up with him. If he took her back to his office, he wasn't sure he could keep his hands to himself. Besides, he really wanted to see if she could mesmerize his audience the way she had him. "The band will be starting a new set in five minutes. I'm sure they can play anything you'd like them to. Just go talk to Louis there and pick something out."

Jessie looked up at the stage, her face paling. She licked her lips.

"Something wrong, doll?"

"No. Of course not. I just wasn't expecting to perform tonight, that's all."

"Well, no better way to see if you like performing than to perform. You need to get a real feel for the stage to see if you want to do this every night."

He watched her, certain she was going to back out. She seemed frightened. He didn't just want her to say yes so he could keep her around. He needed to get closer to her, sure, but he was looking forward to seeing her up on that stage. He was doing a good business, but a sexy vocalist would really class up the joint. And since he needed to compete with The Red Phoenix, and better yet, be enough competition that it would draw the elusive Phoenix himself out, then Tony needed to step up his game and get some better entertainment out on the floor. And if that entertainment was the Phoenix's girl, all the better.

That's if his intended entertainment didn't bolt out his back door. She had taken on a slight shade of green that was a bit worrisome.

"If you've changed your mind…"

"No. No, I'm fine. I'll just go speak to Louis."

Tony nodded, released the hand he was still holding, and gave her a little bow. She visibly firmed up her shoulders and headed to the stage to talk to his bandmaster.

Tony took her place at the table, settling back in his seat. The cigarette girl came by and he snagged a pack of new ciggys off her tray. She lingered for a moment, her eyes offering much more than the wares she was selling, but Tony had no interest. Most of the women working for him would give their eyeteeth for a spot on his arm, or in his bed, more like, but Tony didn't have time for them. He wasn't there for dames. Besides, it was never wise to have a romance with an employee. Things got all kind of complicated when you mixed business and pleasure.

He waved at a waitress and after a moment, she came over and plopped a tumbler of whiskey in front of him. He ignored the barely concealed anger coming from her. He'd already turned down her not-so-subtle offer. Twice. But he was sure she was only after the money she thought a successful speakeasy owner like himself would have.

Unfortunately, all the money he made went right back to the Feds. They were fronting his bills, after all, had set up this whole place in their elaborate scheme to catch the Phoenix. Maybe he could negotiate a nice fat bonus when this was all over. After all, he *was* doing dangerous work for them, going up against not only the Phoenix, but all the other speakeasy owners in town. The Phoenix wasn't the only one who was getting antsy because of Tony's success. Just the other day, he'd caught one of Willie the Weasel's guys sniffing around. If Tony was going to put his life on the line, he figured a little bonus was in order.

All thoughts of Willie the Weasel and the Feds flew out the window the second Jessie stepped up to the microphone. The spotlight flashed on, illuminating her in its glow. She wrapped both hands around the microphone, lightly gripping the metal stand, one finger along the backside of the boxlike mouthpiece.

There were some hoots and hollers from the audience and Tony glanced around, partly pleased at the reaction she was getting and what that could mean for his profits. He wasn't prepared for the anger spiking through him. He nearly rammed an elbow into the man sitting behind him who let loose a particularly loud wolf call. *What is wrong with me?* He wanted his patrons to like her.

He shook it off and downed the whiskey in his glass, slamming the empty down on the table with unnecessary force. The noise of it drew Jessie's attention and she glanced at him, her eyes wide, her luscious lips frowning slightly.

She glanced behind her uncertainly and Louis nodded. The music started, a slow, sultry number. Tony frowned. He recognized the song, but the version he'd heard had been upbeat, campy. Jessie had them playing a different arrangement, one that set the tone for heat and passion before Jessie had even sung a note.

The double bass player plucked a few notes and Jessie's eyes fluttered closed. Her whole demeanor changed as the music flowed over her. She ran her hands down the microphone stand as if it were her lover and then held her arms out to the side as the first notes escaped her mouth.

Tony sat up, his own mouth hanging open. The sensual sounds coming from Jessie captivated everyone in the room. He spared them no notice. As she sang, her body swayed in time to the music. Her hands alternately caressed the microphone, the air, and a few times, her own body, her fingers smoothing the silk of her dress down over her voluptuous hips.

Tony was enthralled. There was no other word for it. She sang like an angel. Well, a seductive temptress of an angel. She opened her eyes and looked right at him, the words of the song seemingly directed at him, meant for him. When she got to the bit where the singer typically did a "boop-boop-a-doop," Jessie made a sort of humming purr sound that hit him like a sucker punch and burned its way down his body. He shifted in his chair. Damn, but the woman was a bearcat. One that had most of the men in the room ready to pounce, if they were feeling anything like him.

When her song was finished, she stood still for a moment, and then the spotlight dimmed. For half a second, there wasn't a sound in the bar. Tony could see Jessie looking around the room, her composure slipping, the self-assuredness she'd assumed while she sang dissipating.

And then a thunderous applause rose. The men, of course, shouted their appreciation, but even the women, far from hating her for drawing their dates' admiration, were joining in the raucous cheering.

Tony stood and jumped onto the stage. He took Jessie's hand and the heat of the spotlight hit them again. He kissed her hand and gave her a little bow and then held his other hand up in the air.

"Ladies and gentlemen! I give you The Corkscrew's new songstress, our very own Jessica Harlan!"

The applause was deafening.

"Give them a bow, sugar. You've earned it."

Jessie glanced up at him and then turned to her audience, gave them a sweeping, if hesitant bow, and then stepped back out of the spotlight. As he was still holding her hand, and had no desire to let go, he stepped back with her.

The band whipped up a rousing Charleston and Tony led Jessie off the stage and through the crowd toward the back of the club.

She tugged on her hand a little. "Where are we going?"

"Back to my office. We've got some business to discuss."

"So, I'm hired?"

"You are indeed, as long as we can come to an agreement on wages and hours."

She didn't need to know that he'd gladly pay her anything she wanted if it kept her on his stage. Tony led her into his office and pulled out a chair for her in front of his desk. Instead of seating himself behind his desk, he perched on the end, not wanting the huge piece of furniture between them.

Jessie watched him, her eyes wary but curious as she took in her surroundings. Tony waited until her attention was back on him before he spoke.

"You've got quite a set of pipes on you." He let his gaze roam over her figure, not hiding the fact that he liked what he saw. "I had no idea you were hiding all that under your butcher's apron."

Jessie's eyebrow rose. "Thanks," she said. Her sardonic tone drew a laugh out of him.

"Sorry. I just mean that I think my patrons will enjoy watching you sing."

"Yeah, I got that."

She looked down, smoothing her hands down her dress. Tony's eyes followed the path her hands took, suddenly wishing her hemline, though already knee length, fell a bit shorter.

"Your song choice was…" Tony trailed off, not sure how to phrase what he wanted to say without making it obvious he'd enjoyed her performance very, very much. Too much.

"I'm sorry. Are you unhappy with my performance?"

Tony looked up, startled. "No. Not unhappy. But…"

Jessie cocked an eyebrow, waiting for him to explain why he was so agitated.

He blew out a breath. "Cripes' sake, woman, were you trying to cause a riot?"

"Excuse me?"

"That song you sang. I'm not sure that was the best choice of opening numbers."

"Why not? It's one of the most popular songs right now. I thought it would be good to start with a bang."

"Yes, but the way you sang it. I've never heard it like that before. Usually the tempo is much more upbeat, fun. But slowing it down like that, singing it like that…"

Jessie's lips pulled into an amused smile. "I didn't realize you were a prude, Mr. Solomon. I'm sorry if I offended your sensibilities."

Tony's mouth dropped open, not sure if he was more amused or offended by the suggestion. "I am not a *prude*, Miss Harlan, but you nearly had every man in there on his knees drooling at your feet."

She crossed her arms and narrowed her eyes. "I thought that was the point," she said, standing and moving away from him.

She was right. It *was* the point. But Tony didn't want any man but himself on his knees before her. And thoughts like that would get him in a lot of trouble he didn't need. He took a breath, carefully weighing his words. Jessie watched him, her blue eyes twinkling. All right. If she wanted to play like that, he could play along. She could act innocent all she liked. No one could put on a show like that and not mean it, at least to some degree. He had no problem with her playing the sex kitten on stage, but if she was going to be coy about it, he'd call her bluff and show her exactly how that song had affected him.

He let his breath out slowly and stood, moving toward her. Jessie stepped back but she was up against the wall. Tony didn't stop until he was nearly pressed against her. His eyes roved over her, lingering on the swell of her hips, the way the dress clung to her breasts.

"When you sang that song, you were looking directly at me."

Now Jessie's mouth dropped open. If she'd been hoping he hadn't noticed, she was foolish. Kind of hard to miss when their eyes had been locked together through the whole song.

"You were in the audience." A weak excuse and he knew she knew it.

"Were you singing that song to me, Jessie? Trying to tell me something, perhaps?"

Jessie *humphed* and tried to sidestep him but he moved with her. "Don't flatter yourself, Mr. Solomon. I was just singing. You happened to be in my line of sight. Yours was the only face I knew in the audience and I was a little nervous. It was only natural for me to look at you. If you'd prefer that I only sing songs the way they were written, I can do that. And I'll give you my set list to approve if you are concerned about my song choices."

Tony studied her. "That won't be necessary. Sing them however you'd like. I will offer a word of advice, though. Unless you want every man out there coming after you like a dog in heat, you might want to make sure you don't lock eyes with anyone but me when you're putting your own delectable spin on things." He drew a finger along her neck and Jessie shivered.

"I'll keep that in mind, Mr. Solomon."

She raised her head, jutting her little chin into the air. Trying to show him she wasn't affected by him. Though all she managed to do was expose more of the creamy expanse of her neck. He longed for a taste of that silky skin. When her teeth scraped over her bottom lip, biting into the soft flesh, Tony sucked in a breath, the sight of it igniting a flash of desire that had his own lips trembling in response.

He mentally gave himself a shake. He was there to do a job, not to ogle a criminal suspect. No matter how charming the dame was. He looked Jessie over again. No. Even if she was some rumrunner's girlfriend, she definitely wasn't the type to go throwing herself at a man. In fact, despite that little show she'd put on up on the stage, he'd be willing to bet she was as innocent as a sweet little lamb. And he'd love to be the one to educate her.

Where the hell did that thought come from? He could just see Jameson's face now. The man would never let him live it down. Tony had been sent in to seduce some information out of her, not be the one seduced. Hell, the woman had been in his office two minutes and in his life barely longer than that, and he was having fantasies about her like some lovesick schoolboy.

Judging by the look on her face, she was very aware of the path his thoughts had taken. And was amused. Tony closed his eyes and backed away from her, moving back to the other side of his desk and taking a seat. Maybe a little distance between them would help.

Nope. The tantalizing smell of her jasmine perfume still reached him, and he didn't think it mattered how far away from her he was, the sight of her still teased parts of him he'd tried hard to ignore for the past few years.

Enough of this. Down to business! He gestured to her vacated chair and she hesitantly sat down again.

"So, Jessie. I'm looking for someone who can sing, six days a week ideally. A few hours each night. I'd pay you thirty dollars a week.

Jessie's eyes widened a bit at that.

"Not enough?" he asked, knowing the price he'd stated was more than fair.

"No, that sounds fine. But I can only come in three days a week. I have…other obligations," she said, not meeting his eyes.

Tony frowned at her to cover the spurt of excitement her words gave him. Coming into his speakeasy wouldn't affect her time at the butcher shop, so she must be referring to her obligations to the Phoenix. And having her available for the Corkscrew might just give him a clue as to when The Red Phoenix was open for business, assuming she was there on the nights she wasn't with Tony.

"All right then. Twenty dollars a week for three nights. Fair?"

Jessie nodded and he continued. "Good. We'll work out a

schedule for you. I have a collection of gowns you may use as your wardrobe and if there is anything you'd like to add to it, just let me know and I'll try and get you what you need. So, do we have an agreement?"

Jessie hesitated, and for a second Tony was afraid she would say no. Luckily, Jessie nodded and stood, holding out her hand.

"Agreed."

He took her hand and shook it, keeping hold of it a tad longer than necessary. She pulled her hand away and stepped back a bit.

"When would you like me to start?"

"Tomorrow night, if that is acceptable."

She nodded. "That will be fine."

"Great. Be here at 11:30 and I'll have someone show you around and get you settled."

"I'll see you then."

Tony watched her walk out of his office and then sat back in his chair, his fingers steepled against his chin. He allowed himself a moment to enjoy the rush of satisfaction that spread through him. The most important part of his plan was now in place. It would be considerably easier to both keep tabs on Jessie Harlan, and get information out of her, if she was at his club, under his eye, than it would be if he had to continually drop in at her shop. With the added bonus of being able to pass along her schedule to Jameson. Their best shot at finding The Red Phoenix open for business and pulling off a successful raid were the days Jessie wasn't scheduled to be at The Corkscrew. That oughta please the little rat bastard.

Thoughts of Jameson were quickly extinguished by the image of Jessie swaying on the stage. The dark, clandestine atmosphere of the club, and the delectable way the little live wire liked to perform, would make cozying up to her less of a challenge, that was for certain. Tony's brow furrowed a bit at that, especially as images of Jessie's full lips, delicious curves, and sultry blue eyes bombarded him. He needed to be careful not to get sucked into his own web. He must remember who was the bad guy. Jessie could not be as innocent as she seemed. She was, at the very least, protecting a criminal, and was possibly just as dirty as the Phoenix was. Tony had his orders. And he'd already paid the price for breaking orders once before. He wouldn't make that mistake again.

No. He had the delectable Miss Harlan right where he wanted her. He just needed to stick to the plan. Maybe this time he'd be able to do his job and no one would get hurt.

Chapter Seven

Jessie looked over her shoulder one last time and then ducked into the alley where the entrance to The Corkscrew was located. The cops had been keeping an eye on her place ever since she'd been with Mario, but she'd only seen them in the vicinity of her shop. Still, she tried to make sure she wasn't being followed when she ventured out, just to be safe. The thought had crossed her mind that she should just lead the coppers right to Tony's doorstep. That would solve the problem of him stealing her competition. It would not, however, give her any answers, and she needed to find out if Tony was working on his own or if he was part of a larger scheme. Either Willie's or the Feds'. Either way, he was a potential threat and she needed to find out just how dangerous to her he was.

She stood at the back entrance of The Corkscrew and adjusted her parcels so she could knock. Three times, pause, two times, pause, then two short rapid knocks. She stood back and waited.

A small window set in the door slid open and a pair of

squinty eyes stared at her.

"Password."

"Swordfish."

The window slammed shut and the door opened, just enough to let her through.

"You Miss Harlan?"

"Yes."

The stocky bald man nodded, jerking his head in the direction of a dimly lit hallway behind him. "The boss is waiting for you. You know where his office is?"

Jessie nodded and he waved her on. The butterflies rioting in her stomach grew more chaotic the closer she got to Tony's closed door. What was she doing? Maude was right. She was insane. Not only was she lying about who she was, a fact that could land her in a world of hurt if Tony found out, (if he was as ruthless as most of the other speakeasy owners), but to gain access to his club, she'd agreed to show up and *sing*. In front of people.

She loved to sing. She really did. She'd belt out any tune — from old church hymns to the hottest nightclub tunes — but only from the safety of her own bathroom. Someplace where no one else could see or hear her.

Though…it had felt great to be on the stage. With the whole band behind her the notes of the music had beat through her, filling her very soul. All she had done was open her mouth and she had been a part of it. She'd almost forgotten about the people who were there, watching her. Almost.

Jessie came to Tony's door and paused, taking a deep breath before she knocked.

"Come in."

Jessie squared her shoulders, popped her chin up a notch, and marched into the office.

Tony looked up, the scowl on his face easing into a grin when he saw her. His pleasure at the sight of her ratcheted her nerves up another notch, but for an entirely different reason. Tony put down the papers he'd been going over and leaned back in his chair.

"Well, Miss Harlan. I'll admit I wasn't sure if you'd show up tonight."

Jessie cocked her head, her brow furrowing. "And why is that?"

Tony shrugged. "You seemed a little…apprehensive."

"That was just nerves. I'm not used to singing in front of people."

"You do realize that that is exactly what this job entails?"

Jessie's lips twitched. "Yes, Mr. Solomon. I'm aware of that."

"Good," Tony said, slapping his hands on his desk as he stood. "Well then, I'll show you around. You didn't quite get the grand tour last time." He slipped an arm around her waist and Jessie stiffened.

"Isn't there someone else who can do that?"

Tony glanced down at her, his eyebrows raised, though there was a slight smile on his full lips.

Jessie blushed. She hadn't meant to say that, and it sounded unforgivably rude. Especially since the man was now her boss. But still…the arm at her waist tightened, making the heat in her cheeks burn even more intensely. Spending time in this man's presence, especially when he insisted on invading her personal space, made her nerves jangle worse than getting up and performing again.

"I only meant I'm sure that you have more important things to do than to squire me around."

"Not at all. I like to make sure my employees are settled in. Besides, I also need to make sure you've got everything you need. You are our main entertainment, doll. If you do well, you could make my joint the most popular in the city. That's worth a few minutes of my time."

Jessie stopped protesting and allowed Tony to lead her down the hallway into a small room that had apparently been designated as a dressing room. Though, as dressing rooms went, it was pretty bare. A rumpled velvet sofa sat against one wall, and a Chinese silk screen portioned off the back of the room, with a small rack of brightly colored dresses along the wall next to it. On her right was a vanity table with a few cosmetics strewn about, and a full-length mirror stood beside that.

Tony looked around, his lips pulling into a frown. "I'm afraid our last singer didn't leave much behind when she left. But if you let me know what you need, I'll make sure you have it."

"No worries. I've brought my own cosmetics."

Tony nodded and waved at the dresses on the rack. "Why don't you go through what's left there and see if anything will work for you."

Jessie deposited her bag on the vanity and draped her dress over the back of the chair. She flipped through the rack of dresses with a growing sense of disappointment. Tony had been right about the last singer not leaving much. Of the four dresses that were left, only one was in relatively decent shape (and by that she meant hole-less and stain-less).

The others were in various states of disrepair. Most were stained and more than a few had cigarette burns in them. Unfortunately, the dress that was wearable was a garish yellow that would look horrible on her. Still, it was the only one she'd willingly let touch her skin, so she drew that one off its hanger.

"You can change behind the screen there." Tony dropped to the sofa and crossed his legs, hooking one foot on the knee of his other leg while he leaned back, draping his arm along the back of the sofa.

Jessie's mouth dropped open. "You want me to change

while you are in here?"

"You'll be behind the screen. I assure you I can't see anything. I need to see how it looks on you and staying put is a lot more expedient than having me wait out in the hall like some bag boy."

Jessie considered protesting, but he was right. She would be hidden enough behind the screen and besides, Tony didn't seem like the type of man she could easily persuade. She sighed and stomped behind the screen, removing her own clothing and slipping the dress over her head as quickly as she could.

The minute it slid over her chest, she knew it wouldn't work. Whoever had worn the dress before had been at least two sizes smaller, and a great deal more flat chested. She grabbed the hem and tugged it down over her curves, squeezing herself into it like it was a sausage casing. She got all the important parts covered, but just barely. And the material pulled so tightly over her body that it was barely decent.

She glanced down at herself and revised that thought. It wasn't anywhere near decent.

"How's it going?" Tony asked.

"Um…I don't think this one will work."

"Well, come on out here and let me see."

"That's really not necessary, I assure you—"

"Baloney. Come on out."

Jessie sighed and stepped out from behind the screen, fighting the urge to cover her breasts with her arms. The material barely contained them and it was stretched so tightly, too deep a breath would expose all her bits and pieces.

Tony's mouth opened slightly as he took her in, but he didn't say anything. Jessie wasn't sure if he was horrified at how ghastly she looked or if it was something else. Finally, he looked away, shifting uncomfortably on the couch, and waved her back behind the screen.

"No, you're right. That one won't do at all. What about the others?"

"They look to be all the same size."

"Well then. We'll have to remedy that first thing tomorrow. But for tonight…"

"I've brought something I can wear tonight."

"Oh. Excellent. All right then. When you're ready, come back to my office and I'll introduce you to the rest of the band members and you can discuss your set numbers with them. I'd like you on the stage by midnight."

Jessie nodded, her mouth suddenly dry. *What have I gotten myself into? Set numbers?*

Tony gave her a wink and pulled the door closed behind him. Jessie leaned against it a moment.

"Pull yourself together, Harlan. Good grief, it's only a few songs."

Jessie shook herself off, grabbed the dress she'd borrowed from Maude from the back of the chair, and went behind the screen. She peeled the hideous yellow dress off and slipped into her own dress. The silk slipped across her skin like fresh, warm cream and hugged her curves in all the right places. She felt like the absolute cat's pajamas in it. The neckline was lower than she usually dared to wear, but for a nightclub singer, it was perfect.

She pulled out her cosmetic bag and refreshed her makeup. She ran the pencil along her brows, dabbed a bit more rouge on her cheeks and smeared Maude's bright red lipstick across her lips. The overall effect was very nice. Lighter, she was sure, than Maude would want, but for Jessie it was more than enough. She patted the waves of her hair back into place, securing the rhinestone and feather headband that had been made for the dress across her forehead.

She took a look in the full-length mirror, turning this way and that. The deep sapphire blues and luminous greens of the beaded peacock feathers on the dress brought out the color of her eyes, making them brilliantly bright in her pale face. She pinched her cheeks, trying to help the rouge along, and put her hands on her hips.

"Well, that'll have to do." She took one last deep breath and headed out.

Tony's door was open so she gave it a quick knock and pushed it the rest of the way.

"Mr. Solomon? I'm ready."

Tony glanced up and froze. For a moment, Jessie was afraid she'd spilled some powder or something on her dress. But a quick perusal alleviated that worry. Maybe she wasn't fancy enough?

"Do I look all right?"

Tony's mouth snapped shut and he looked back down, shuffling the papers on his desk. "Yes. Fine."

He cleared his throat and Jessie smiled, a warm confidence ebbing through her and soothing her rattled nerves. The papers in his hand were backward and his pen was upside down. Apparently, she looked more than *fine*.

Tony abandoned his paperwork and came around the desk, looping her arm through his.

"Let's go meet the band."

Jessie tried to calm the nerves building again in her gut. It was almost show time.

Tony led her into a small room behind the stage where the band members were lounging.

"Fellas, this is our new singer, Jessica Harlan. Jessie, you spoke with Louis last night, but this is the rest of your band."

Jessie waved shyly as the men stood and came to greet her.

Louis stepped up front and shook her hand. "Glad to see you again, miss. If you can sing like you did last night, we'll bring the house down in no time."

Jessie flushed with pleasure and returned his handshake with genuine delight.

"I'm very pleased to meet you all," Jessie said, relieved that they were so welcoming.

"You definitely class up the joint," Louis said.

The other men nodded in agreement.

"We've been asking Tony to get another singer in here since Ida split. Glad he finally decided to give in. We can play all right on our own, but a joint like this really needs a good set of pipes to get swinging."

Their enthusiasm went a long way to putting Jessie at ease. "Well, I'll try my best to do you proud."

Tony squeezed her arm. "I'm going to go check out our crowd tonight. Jessie, why don't you discuss the songs you'd like to sing. I will probably be gone for the night by the time you are done. But we have a few errands we need to run tomorrow. Can you get someone to watch your shop for you?"

"Errands?"

"Yes. Your shop? Can you get away for a few hours?"

"Um, yes, I have someone who can manage things for a little while."

"Excellent. I'll pick you up at ten o'clock then."

Jessie nodded, bemused. What *errands* could he possibly need to run with her?

She watched Tony walk away and couldn't help but admire the view. The man looked as good going as coming. She bit her lip, shocked at her own thoughts but unable to keep them from venturing into territory that made her skin tingle.

Louis cleared his throat and Jessie turned to him, though she couldn't bring herself to look him in the eye. Luckily, he took pity on her and kept his observations to himself.

Jessie was happy to discover the band knew all the songs she wanted to sing, even a few of the more obscure ones. And they were happy to try the new arrangements she suggested. They came up with a set list and a schedule. She'd sing for half an hour and then would get a break for fifteen or twenty minutes. The boss, as the men called Tony, usually opened the bar for business around eleven o'clock and kept it going until three a.m., so Jessie would need to arrive by ten thirty, at the latest, in order to get ready.

Fatigue lapped at her. She'd been up since four o'clock that morning to accept a delivery of beef and she'd worked hard all day at the shop. Maude and Joe would make sure The Red Phoenix ran smoothly on the days she wasn't there, but she had to make an appearance some days as well. It just wouldn't be smart to be open only on the days she wasn't at The Corkscrew, so there were going to be times when she'd be dropping in at her own club early, going to The Corkscrew, and then closing up shop at The Red Phoenix. She was definitely going to have to hire some temporary help if she was going to keep up the double life without keeling over. A girl had to sleep sometime.

The band took their places. Jessie closed her eyes and took a few calming breaths. All those people watching her sent her stomach in a tailspin, but once the music began, she'd be all right.

She was thrilled when the crowd cheered and hollered at the end of every song, and she and the band kept things roaring until the boys had to start kicking people out. And through it all, she could feel Tony's eyes following her every move. She'd never felt so on display. But when he was the one watching, Jessie didn't mind as much. A girl could get addicted to his kind of attention. And that was something Jessie would have to guard herself against very carefully. Because she had a feeling that Tony Solomon would be a very hard habit to kick.

Chapter Eight

Jessie looked at Tony as if he'd just grown a second head. "You are *not* taking me shopping."

"Why ever not?

"Because…because…it's just not done! Besides, I'm perfectly capable of choosing my own clothing. I don't need you to dress me."

"I beg to differ. My clientele expects a certain look, and nothing you have quite fits the bill."

Jessie looked down at the pile of dresses she'd dragged out of her closet and tried to be offended on behalf of her clothing, but Tony was right. Her clothes were, for the most part, sturdy and sensible. Aside from a few party dresses and Maude's slinky little number that she'd worn the night before, nothing in her wardrobe was suitable for a nightclub singer.

"Be that as it may, I cannot allow you to purchase clothing for me."

"Who's being the prude now?"

Jessie gasped and pinned Tony with a glare that should have had him withering on her kitchen floor, but instead prompted a bark of laughter from him. "I'm not making an indecent proposal. I'm merely trying to ensure that my employee is properly outfitted to perform her duties. Think of the clothing as a uniform, if it makes you feel better."

A uniform, huh? That actually did make Jessie feel a bit better. Truthfully, she was thrilled at the thought of a closet full of shiny new dresses. She just worried over what it might mean to accept them from Tony. She'd enjoyed singing in his club more than she'd expected and hopefully she'd be able to get the goods on him—such as, if he and Willie were partners. Or he and Jameson. Or whoever else he might be in cahoots with. Until she found out differently, he was the enemy and that was something she'd do very well to keep in mind. She did *not* want to engage in any extracurricular activities with her handsome new boss.

Well, that wasn't entirely true. Jessie's traitorous cheeks flamed at the memory of Tony's finger drifting down the column of her neck. The heat in his gaze when he stared at her. The man in question was looking at her with a quizzical expression and her blush deepened. She turned away from him, but judging from his smug smile, he'd seen her reaction and knew exactly what it was about.

Oh, applesauce! She was being ridiculous. "Fine. Let's get this over with, then."

She grabbed her coat, slammed her hat on her head, yanked her gloves over her hands, and marched to the door.

Tony shook his head. "I've never met a dame who had to be forced into dolling up."

Jessie stopped on the sidewalk and waited for Tony to open the door to his automobile. She didn't say another word until he'd slid onto the seat beside her. She knew she was being surly and she couldn't quite put her finger on why. His request wasn't unreasonable. After all, it was his club and she would be entertaining there. He had every right to make sure she looked the part.

She sighed. She might hate it, but she admitted when she was in the wrong. Maybe she could cut him a little break. For now.

"I apologize if I seem out of sorts. I'm just used to fending for myself. I don't like being in anyone's debt and you buying me dresses hits a little too close to the mark."

And it was oddly personal, for a man she wasn't involved with, to be buying her clothing. But she didn't add that.

Tony nodded. "I can understand that. Well, how about we say the dresses are costumes that belong to the club. For as long as you sing there, you are welcome to them. But should you move on, they will be left behind for the next girl. Would that make you feel better about all this?"

A sliver of disappointment settled in her gut. What he offered was the perfect solution. He got to dress her to his heart's content and she didn't have to be morally offended by the situation. She mentally kicked herself in the keister for turning down ownership of the new clothes.

But she couldn't very well decline now, after the stink she'd raised. "That would suit me just fine, thank you."

Tony smiled again, as though he knew exactly what she was thinking, and turned his attention back to the road. He turned onto the main thoroughfare, cutting off a delivery truck in the process.

Jessie just barely managed to keep from shrieking, emitting instead a high-pitched, strangled gasp while she clung to the frame of the car, praying her heart would stay in her chest and her breakfast would stay in her stomach.

Tony looked at her and raised an eyebrow at her white-knuckled grasp on the dashboard. "Is something wrong?"

"That truck almost plowed right into us."

Tony frowned, obviously not sure what she meant. He barreled up to a line of cars waiting at an intersection, not applying the brakes nearly fast enough for Jessie. She slammed her feet on the floorboards, irrationally hoping she could somehow slow the vehicle from where she sat. She released a deep breath, trying to keep from screaming at him like a harpy, and instead closed her eyes. Perhaps if she couldn't see the near collisions that seemed to be Tony's way of driving, she would be able to get to the shop without making a complete fool of herself.

"Are you all right?" Tony asked.

"Fine," Jessie bit out.

"What's the matter? Don't you like riding in an automobile?"

"Not particularly, no."

Tony laughed and revved the engine, gunning the car through the intersection. "Why ever not?"

"If God had meant for us to go barreling toward each other at forty miles per hour we'd have been born with wheels on our feet."

Tony's laughter rang through the car. Jessie turned her head, ignoring him. Honestly, she didn't mind the occasional ride and went along with Charlie and Joe on deliveries often enough. But they didn't drive the way Tony did, and being surrounded by the sturdy delivery van seemed safer than being encased in all the glass and fancy upholstery of Tony's auto.

"I'll slow down a bit," Tony assured her.

Jessie let out another breath and her heart finally slowed to a normal beat. "Thank you."

In no time at all, they were parked in front of a sweet little dress shop that Jessie had always admired but had never bothered to enter. Tony hopped out to open the door for her. He escorted her through the big double doors and into the boutique.

What followed next was a morning that Jessie would never

have dreamed of, even in her wildest fantasies. Tony settled himself on a couch in front of three huge dressing mirrors and waited like a king for Jessie to parade each selection before him. She was like some overgrown peacock strutting about in plumage every shade of the rainbow.

But oh, what wonderful feathers. She tried everything from short little numbers covered in tassels and rhinestones to slinky confections that fell to the floor like liquid silk pouring down her body. And it wasn't just the clothes. Each dress had to have matching shoes, handbags, rhinestones, feathers, and headbands for her hair, and glittering brooches, armbands, and rings. Jessie was swimming in a sea of silk and glitter and despite herself, she loved every minute of it.

Tony picked out several dresses, along with their matching accessories, of course. And they were all beautiful. But it was the last gown that Jessie absolutely fell in love with. The cream colored silk hugged her body like a second skin, outlining every curve she had. The wide straps on the shoulders dipped into a low draped neckline that showed more than a hint of ample cleavage, and the back was simply scandalous. It hung low enough that she wouldn't be able to wear any underthings with it. She'd never worn anything like it before and the thought of wearing it on stage in front of everyone made her mouth dry up like she was sucking cotton.

But when she stepped out from behind the changing curtain and stood in front of Tony, his eyes widened. His mouth opened slightly, his gaze traveling from her head to her toes and back up again. Her smile spread slowly until she knew she was all but beaming at him. There was something incredibly empowering about striking a man dumb. She did a little turn so he could get the full effect.

His teeth scraped over his bottom lip and Jessie froze, the sight of it sending a bolt of heat straight to her core. She licked her lips, her mouth gone suddenly dry.

Tony cleared his throat, breaking the spell, and Jessie looked away, trying to compose herself.

"That one as well," he instructed the woman helping them.

"Jessica Harlan? Is that you?"

Jessie groaned and turned to the old woman who approached them with a smile. "Mrs. Finch, how lovely to see you."

She gave Mrs. Finch a hug and then braced herself. Mrs. Finch had been her neighbor for almost as long as she could remember, and had been acquainted with her father for even longer than that. She was very straitlaced and uptight, even carried her Bible in her purse, though Jessie could never figure out why, because the woman had it memorized and made sure everyone around her knew it.

Mrs. Finch looked Jessie up and down, her face puckering more by the second. "Well, I know I'm no expert on what constitutes fashion these days," she said, drawing her brown wool coat about her like she was donning armor for battle. "But I can say with certainty that your poor mother is turning in her grave right now at the thought of her little girl wearing such a…a frock as that."

Jessie didn't see how Mrs. Finch could say that with any degree of certainty since the woman had never met Jessie's mother. Jessie herself barely remembered her. Still, she resisted the urge to cover herself as Mrs. Finch continued to look at her as though she were the most offensive piece of trash ever to cross her path. "I don't think it's that bad, Mrs. Finch. This style is all the rage now."

"More's the pity, if you ask me."

Jessie hadn't, but she refrained from mentioning that. Not that it mattered. Mrs. Finch wasn't paying attention to her anymore. She'd caught sight of Tony lounging on the sofa, watching them with an amused gleam in his eye. Jessie tried to communicate a warning, pleading with her eyes for him to play dumb, pretend he didn't know her. Anything to keep the woman from knowing who he was and why he was sitting there watching Jessie parade around in such obviously immoral clothing.

Mrs. Finch's beady little eyes darted from Tony to Jessie and back again, her face growing more puckered and disapproving with every second. Then the shopgirl came up to Tony with a stack of boxes and Jessie closed her eyes, wishing a giant hole would open up right there and swallow her whole.

"Here you are, Mr. Solomon. We can deliver the rest of your purchases if you'd prefer not to take them with you now. And this as well," she said, gesturing to the offending material on Jessie's body and looking back and forth between Jessie and Tony.

Mrs. Finch fairly sputtered with indignation. She rounded on Jessie, her hands on her hips, her pearls nearly popping off the vein bulging in her neck. "Jessica Marie Harlan, all I can do is thank my lucky stars that your poor father isn't alive to see what you've become." She seized her hand and pulled her close. "I blame myself. I should have made sure you were looked after. It's not right, you there at that shop all by yourself, without a proper chaperone. I told myself time and time again, 'Thelma, you need to go over and make sure that girl is taken care of, and finds someone to do her right.' But did I listen? No, I did not. And look what's come of it." She shot Tony a look of pure venom.

Jessie was afraid to glance at him and when she did she wished she hadn't. He looked like he was having a devil of a time keeping from rolling on the floor with laughter. Jessie added her own glare to Mrs. Finch's. It was *not* funny!

Mrs. Finch apparently agreed. "I don't see what you find so amusing, young man. You should be ashamed of yourself, taking this poor innocent young girl and corrupting her for your own vile purposes. Why I never—"

Tony stood and held up a hand. "I'm afraid you've misunderstood."

"Have I?" the woman said, as she crossed her arms over her rather ample chest. "I don't see a ring on her finger and even if there was one, no decent man would want his wife traipsing about in that…that…"

"Of course, you are right. But you see, I'm looking for a few presents for my sister. She's coming into town soon and I wanted to surprise her. Only I have no idea what size she wears or what she might like. I met this delightful young lady only a few moments ago and quite literally begged her to aid me. She looks to be the same size as my sister and she agreed, reluctantly, I promise you, to try on a few things. Just to help me out."

Mrs. Finch kept him pinned with a glare, waiting to see if he'd crack under the pressure. Tony smiled at her so angelically that Jessie had to turn her head to keep from laughing. Mrs. Finch finally turned back to Jessie.

"Is that true?"

"Yes, ma'am. I'd never wear such a thing myself, of course. And would certainly never let a gentleman buy me something so intimate as clothing."

Mrs. Finch nodded her head. "Quite right. Well, that does give me some relief, I must say. You always were such a good girl," she said, patting Jessie's cheek. "Now, go take that garment off. *I* will help the young man find something suitable for his sister."

Jessie watched dumbstruck as Tony offered Mrs. Finch his arm and began escorting her from rack to rack of clothing, thanking her so profusely that Jessie was sure Mrs. Finch would see right through him.

Apparently, Tony was a better actor than Jessie gave him credit for, because by the time she came out of the dressing room, Mrs. Finch was flushed and pink as a schoolgirl, gazing up at Tony with a goofy grin that Jessie had never seen on the woman's face.

He was laying a drab brown frock on the counter that looked like it belonged more around a pile of potatoes than on a woman, but Mrs. Finch was beaming with pride at the wonderfully sensible dress she'd found for Tony's "sister."

Tony thanked her again and bent to kiss her hand. Mrs. Finch flushed bright pink and hurried over to give Jessie a parting hug. "Now, my dear, you don't be a stranger, you hear. I'll be sure to drop in on you more frequently, make sure all is well."

"Oh, Mrs. Finch, that's very kind, but it isn't necessary. I'm doing quite well, I assure you."

"Oh tosh, it'll be my pleasure. And it's the least I can do."

She hurried out with a wave at both of them.

Jessie turned to Tony, her eyebrow raised. But before she could say anything, Tony took the dress from her and beamed. "I'll just go settle the bill."

Jessie opened her mouth, but for the life of her couldn't scrape together two words.

A moment later, Tony returned and held out his arm. "The valet is bringing the car around. Shall we?"

Jessie tucked her hand into the crook of his elbow. "You're a very accomplished actor, Mr. Solomon."

He shrugged. "I can be, I suppose. If the occasion calls for it."

"*Hmm*, I'll have to keep that in mind."

He glanced at her, his brow slightly furrowed. But before he could answer, the valet pulled up in the car.

Tony opened the door for Jessie and she slid across the leather seats. She was grateful he'd been able to rescue her from Mrs. Finch. But no doubt about it, the man could spin a tale and had no qualms about doing it. She'd have to keep a very close eye on the multi-talented Mr. Solomon.

Chapter Nine

Jessie rushed into her office at The Red Phoenix, her arms so laden with boxes she could barely push aside the bookcase that hid her secret entrance into the club. A knock sounded on the door to her office just as she entered. She dumped the boxes on the floor, shoved the bookcase back into place, and went to answer the door.

Joe stood there, patiently waiting with his hat in his hand.

"Joe, I'm so sorry. Come in."

Joe followed her in, sitting in the chair in front of her desk. Jessie slumped into her own chair and laid her head on the desk. Joe waited patiently until Jessie sat up, rubbing her eyes.

"You're working too hard. You need to let me help you more and not just at the shop. I can do more here," Joe said, his kind voice reminding her of her father. Though when she opened her eyes to look at him, the resemblance disappeared.

Her father had been tall, thin, and very bald. Joe on the other hand, still sported a full head of silver-tinged black hair, and was built like a Buddha idol Jessie had once seen. He wasn't much taller than Jessie herself, but what he lacked in height, he more than made up for in girth.

"You do too much for me already."

Joe shook his head. "It's not right, you working yourself to the bone to pay off your daddy's debt. Your daddy's dead and gone. His debt should have gone with him."

Jessie gave him a tired smile. "I agree. But Willie, unfortunately, does not."

"That Willie is an evil man."

"Again, I agree. But he loaned my father the money when he needed it and he certainly doesn't care that he died. He wants his money. And since the shop still isn't pulling in enough to keep it running *and* pay the debt…well, let's just be thankful I found the stash of gin so I could open this place," she said.

"Don't we have enough yet? Business has been good, here and at the shop."

"It has been. Very good. But if we were to close The Red Phoenix now, I'm not sure the shop is stable enough to keep running just yet. Not in addition to paying off the rest of the debt."

She didn't add that she couldn't bear the thought of having to let Joe go if she couldn't keep their finances going. He'd come to work at the shop when Jessie had been about twelve or so, and when her dad had died Joe had stayed on to help Jessie run things. Without him, the shop would have gone under long ago and she couldn't let him down now.

Joe frowned slightly. "You know you don't have to worry about me. I'll be all right, even if you weren't able to keep me on."

Jessie smiled. "I know you would be, Joe. But you aren't the only one whose livelihood is on the line. What about Charlie? And Maude? Jobs seem to be getting scarcer by the day."

Jessie knew that Charlie hadn't been able to find anything

permanent that would keep bread on his table and his bills paid until Jessie had hired him. Maude, too, had been at the end of her rope when Jessie had offered her the job singing at The Red Phoenix. If The Red Phoenix were to close, what would Maude do? Oh, she'd have no problem getting hired at another speakeasy, but most of them were run by Capone's or Willie's men. Not exactly a great working environment for a single lady. At least Maude was safe at The Red Phoenix.

So, as tired as Jessie was, as frazzled as she was keeping The Red Phoenix open and having to deal with cops and prohi agents—*and* singing at The Corkscrew—she just couldn't close the speakeasy yet. Too many people were depending on her for their living, either through the speakeasy or the butcher shop. She had to ride it out a little longer until she had all her debts paid off and enough stockpiled to keep things running should business slow down again.

"You take on too much, Jessie." Joe patted her arm. "You don't have to do it all alone, you know."

Jessie smiled and covered his hand with her own. With her dad gone, Joe had stepped into the father role. Aside from Maude, he was the only one Jessie trusted. It was nice to have someone to share that burden with, though even Joe didn't know everything about the speakeasy. Where the main stash of gin was, for instance, or the location of the private door Jessie used. Jessie tried to operate on a need-to-know basis, just in case any of her people were picked up by the Feds or one of her rivals. They couldn't reveal secrets they didn't know.

And as much as Jessie would love the help, she wanted to keep Joe and Maude as ignorant as possible. The less they knew, the less involved they were, the safer they were.

"I know, Joe. And I can't tell you how much I appreciate the offer. I promise if it gets to be too much, I'll consider it."

"Uh, huh," Joe mumbled, pinning her with an exasperated

look that said he knew she needed help and was just being too stubborn to ask for it.

Jessie smiled. She loved the old guy. "Actually, now that you mention it, I was thinking of having you help out a bit more. And Charlie too, if he can."

"Of course. You need Charlie to take more hours in the shop?"

"If he could, just for a few weeks, and I'll need you to run things here for a few extra nights a week."

Joe's brow crinkled. "We're happy to help, of course. It's about time you let us take on more." He folded his arms and stared at her. "You mind if I ask why you're letting us help all of a sudden?"

"You worry too much, Joe," she said, standing and giving him a hug.

"Not enough, I'd say. Someone needs to worry about you now and then."

"Here," she said, smiling and handing him several folders. "The receipts for the past month and the time sheets for the staff. If you could go over my figures, make sure everything is correct, I'll get the cash so you can divvy up the payroll."

Joe nodded and took the files out to the bar area where he could spread everything out.

As soon as the door closed behind him, Jessie slid down in her chair a bit, until her head rested on the back of the chair, and let her eyes close. The stress weighing on her shoulders eased a little. Joe would run things at The Red Phoenix. The shop would be in the capable hands of Charlie. He was only nineteen, not too much younger than she was, though at times he seemed like an over-eager puppy. To be fair, that was mostly when Maude was in the shop. Jessie couldn't blame him. Maude was divine. Other than that, Charlie had a good level head on his shoulders. Jessie could trust him.

In any case, right now, she could spare a few minutes to

relax.

Someone knocked on her door and Jessie stood up and laughed. Looked like quiet time was over.

• • •

Tony slammed the envelope down on his desk and took a deep breath. It wouldn't do to go breaking everything in his office. That would only cost him more money. Money he wouldn't have unless he could pinch the damn Phoenix and get his career going again. He'd been having fun living on the Feds' dime, but that clambake wasn't going to last for long, especially if he couldn't deliver what they were looking for and soon. The initial month they'd given had come and gone. It had taken much longer to get things set up and get him established at The Corkscrew than they'd anticipated. His timeframe had been extended, but the Feds would run out of patience eventually.

And right now, the only thing he had going for him was that Jessie was working at The Corkscrew. Maybe that meant she wasn't as close to the Phoenix as they'd thought. Or that they'd had a falling out. Then again, she could be working both sides. Or maybe it meant nothing at all.

Ton sighed and slumped into his chair, rubbing his hands over his face before sliding down so he could rest his head on the back of his chair. He stared at a water spot on the ceiling and for the millionth time, he cursed himself for letting his life fall so completely apart.

Two years ago, he'd been a highly respected detective on the fast track to career glory. He'd brought in more criminals and closed more cases than anyone else on the force. He'd not only been the best at his job, he'd loved it too. Not something every man could say. He'd had it good. A nice apartment, a closet full of good suits, and a beautiful dame on his arm.

Lucille. Now, just her name made him cringe. He'd been a goner for her, one of those guys other guys mocked. He'd have done anything for her. And had. Which was why when she had come to him with a tip on where he could find Willie the Weasel's newest bootlegging operation, he hadn't questioned it. All she had to do was blink up at him with her big brown eyes and say, "Trust me," and he had turned into a total sap. She was his girl.

Or so he had thought.

Turned out she had really been Willie's girl, and that tip she'd given him was baloney, a smoke screen to keep the cops busy while Willie set up his new operation somewhere else. When Tony had realized he'd been double-crossed, he hadn't believed it, at first. Hadn't believed that Lucille had set him up like that. His captain told him to bring her in, but he couldn't do it. Couldn't put her in cuffs and drag her into the precinct like some crook.

He'd been sure she'd been coerced somehow, threatened. Thought if he could get her alone, talk to her, he could find out the truth.

The truth had been that she was a lying, no good floozy that he should have run from the second he'd clapped eyes on her. But he hadn't wanted to believe that either. He had gone charging in after her, against his captain's orders, still not believing she'd done him wrong until the gun had rung out and one of Willie's guys had put a bullet through his partner's head.

He had lost everything because of her. His job, the respect of his colleagues, his self-respect. His partner.

That's what kept him up at night. His partner was dead because he hadn't been able to see past a pair of pretty eyes and soft lips. He deserved the life he lived now because he shouldn't even *be* alive. It should have been him who had gone down that night, not Stan. He only thanked God that

Stan hadn't had a family. No more lives that would have been ruined.

If it hadn't been for Tony's mother, he would be well on his way to drinking himself to death by now. Prohibition or no Prohibition. Hell, he'd been a cop. He knew where the speakeasies were. He could have done it and would have welcomed the numbness that came with too much booze.

But his ma didn't have anyone else. She needed him. So here he was. Trying to scrape by doing private investigations for rich men who couldn't keep their wives from sleeping with the gardener and rich women who thought their maids might be stealing from them. He made enough to get by, but it was a near thing every month. And his ma deserved better than what he could give her right now.

What he needed was for his little songbird to start singing. He didn't like the idea of using her, but he had no illusions that she was an innocent in this game, though at times he could swear she was. No. Even if she wasn't in as deep as Jameson thought, she had to be involved, somehow. She had information he needed, information that was illegal to keep, and he wasn't going to let some gangster's moll get in the way of getting his life back.

Tony opened his bottom drawer and pulled out the battered, coffee-stained file. He flipped it open. Jessie's picture stared up at him.

She'd been brought in half a dozen times before Jameson had come to him, but she didn't seem to know anything. Anything useful, anyway. However, something about her answers seemed off to Tony. He wished he had been in on the interrogations. He was good at reading people, their reactions, body language. He could usually tell when someone was lying. He shied away from the memory of Lucille and focused on what he'd read in Jessie's files.

Officer: Who is the man known as the Phoenix?

Jessica: I don't know any man by that name.

Officer: Have you ever been to a speakeasy known as The Red Phoenix?

Jessica: Yes.

Officer: Can you take us there?

Jessica: No.

Officer: So you are refusing to tell us the location of the speakeasy?

Jessica: You didn't ask me where the location was.

Officer: Where is the location of the speakeasy?

Jessica: In Chicago.

Officer: We are aware of that. Surely you can be more specific. Can you tell us where exactly it is? What street it is located on?

Jessica: Not with any degree of certainty, no.

Officer: Why not?

Jessica: It's not really on a street.

Officer: If it is located in this city, it must have an address.

Jessica: If it does, I have no idea what it is.

Officer: Fine. We'll come back to that one. Who supplies the

Phoenix?

Jessica: No one.

Officer: He must have a supplier.

Jessica: Why is that?

Officer: He must get the booze he sells from somewhere. Does he run it from Canada, across Lake Michigan or Huron maybe, or is he bootlegging over land from another city? Make it himself?

Jessica: The only person I ever knew who made their own liquor was my father. And he's dead.

Officer: You said the Phoenix does not have a supplier, which must mean he makes his own liquor. Where is his operation?

Jessica: I can't tell you that.

Officer: Can't or won't.

Jessica: Can't.

Officer: Young lady, if you do not answer my questions we will charge you with obstruction of justice. You'll go to jail.

Jessica: I am answering your questions. I can't help it if you don't like my answers.

Officer: You are not answering my questions.

Jessica: I have answered every question you've asked.

Officer: Where is the Phoenix's booze operation?

Jessica: The Phoenix doesn't have one.

Tony rubbed his hand over his eyes, torn between frustration and flat-out laughing. The woman had really taken the poor officer for a ride, though she was correct. She had technically answered every question she'd been asked. Tony had to admire the officer's restraint in not strangling her, though. He turned back to the statements.

Officer: Can you tell us what days the speakeasy is open?

Jessica: No.

Officer: Why not?

Jessica: Because it always changes.

Officer: But the Phoenix tells you what days it'll be open so you can pass the information along. Is that right?

Jessica: No.

Officer: No, he doesn't give you the information?

Jessica: Yes.

Officer: Yes he does?

Jessica: No.

Officer: You said yes.

Jessica: That's correct.

Officer: What's correct? Can you clarify your answer?

Jessica: Certainly. What was the question again?

Tony finally gave in to the urge and laughed. He'd love to be the one interrogating the little bearcat. A quick mental flash of her sparkling eyes, full, smiling lips and soft, luscious curves gave him a few other ideas of what he'd like to do the next time they were alone. But he pushed those thoughts away and focused on the case at hand.

The interview had gone on along these lines for a while before the interrogator had given up and let her go. They didn't have enough to hold her and she wasn't giving up any information. She never admitted that she knew the Phoenix, but the way she answered other questions made it obvious she did know the man, or at least details of his operation. Though according to her, the man didn't have a supplier nor did he make his own booze. Which left the question, if he doesn't buy it or make it, where is he getting the booze he sells? Perhaps he'd stolen it. That could explain why Willie was so interested.

It'd be much easier if he could just ask her what he wanted to know. Subtlety wasn't his strong suit. He preferred to be straightforward and this subterfuge bit wasn't sitting well with him. He had to admit, now that he was getting to know her, he couldn't understand why she'd be mixed up with a man like the Phoenix. She didn't seem the type. She'd seemed more comfortable swinging a knife in her butcher shop than draped in tassels and feathers onstage in the speakeasy.

Then again, she'd been with Russo, though by all accounts it hadn't lasted long. But now she was mixed up with yet another bootlegger. As incongruous as it was, she must be hiding the man for a reason. Maybe she'd been threatened, though nothing about her indicated that she was afraid. She had come into the precinct when summoned. She had answered questions calmly and coolly. She never seemed to get ruffled. That suggested to Tony that she was willingly hiding something, not being coerced into lying.

She probably *was* the Phoenix's dame. Lying to protect her rum running lover. Which made her just as bad as the criminal.

Tony didn't want to examine why that thought made his gut turn like he'd ingested a vat of rotgut. In the end, it didn't matter. He had a job to do, and he was going to do it. No matter how he felt about it.

Chapter Ten

Tony paced the hallway near The Corkscrew's entrance and checked his watch for the umpteenth time. She was only a few minutes late. *Make that nineteen minutes*, Tony thought, shoving his pocket watch back into his vest. There were any number of reasons she might be running behind. It was raining. Maybe she couldn't get a cab. Maybe there was an issue at the butcher shop that needed her attention.

Or maybe she'd decided she didn't want to come back. Though surely she would have sent word. She wouldn't just not show up. Unless someone was keeping her from coming. If the Phoenix had decided he didn't want his girl playing spy for him anymore, or if he thought something else was going on, or if Willie had gotten to her…

Anxiety sat like a lead ball in Tony's gut and every second that ticked by made it grow and fester. When the secret knock sounded on the door, Tony jumped, pushing aside his doorman so he could slide back the eyehole himself. Jessie's upturned face looked back at him and he yanked the door open before she could utter the password.

She squeaked in surprise when he grasped her arm and hauled her inside.

"Where have you been?" he said, trying to keep the concern from his voice.

Her eyebrow rose a notch and he tried to rein it in. He had no right to act like some fretful lover, but he could be the disapproving boss. Tony crossed his arms and glared down at her. "You're late."

"I know, I'm terribly sorry," Jessie said, her brilliant smile undermining her words. The little minx didn't seem at all sorry. She turned and hurried down the hall, calling back another apology over her shoulder. She seemed to be in remarkably good spirits, something that he might enjoy under normal circumstances. But after spending nearly half an hour worried about her well-being, he found her good mood irritating. He followed right on her heels, pushing through the dressing room door she tried to close in his face.

She looked startled but didn't protest as he followed her inside. She dropped her belongings on the vanity table and went behind the screen to change.

Tony took a deep breath and sank onto the sofa. She didn't appear in any way harmed or upset. Looks like he'd let his imagination run wild for no reason.

"Are you going to tell me why you are twenty minutes late or do I have to guess?"

Tony knew he sounded like an ass but the urge to haul her into his arms and assure himself she was whole and unharmed was almost too great to resist. Better to keep them both in their places and play up the disgruntled boss routine.

"I'm sorry," Jessie said again, her voice momentarily muffled.

Tony gritted his teeth, the sudden vision of her raising her arms to let her silky dress flow down over her supple body invading his mind.

She stepped out from behind the screen and took a seat at the vanity, reaching for her hairbrush.

"There were a few issues at my clu—shop that needed my attention and by the time I'd finished, it was pouring rain and I had a devil of a time getting a cab."

Tony hadn't missed the slight pause before "shop" but let it go. For now. He released an exasperated sigh. "You need to get an automobile."

Jessie snorted and applied some lipstick. "I couldn't afford one of those machines even if I wanted one."

Hell, he'd buy her one if it would save him another evening like he'd just had, even if he had to steal the money to do it.

"Why wouldn't you want one? It'd save you having to rely on cabs." *And giving me a heart attack when you don't show up on time*, he added silently.

"I'll ride in them when necessary," she said, pressing some fresh powder to her face, "and have even enjoyed it a few times, when they are not driven by a maniac, that is." She gave him a pointed look and he couldn't help but smile at her. "But I have no intention of ever *driving* one. I'll stick with a cab when necessary and my own two feet whenever possible, thank you very much."

She jumped up, bent down to look in the mirror and gave her hair one last pat, then spun toward the door. "Come on, boss, get a wiggle on!" She flashed him a huge, intoxicating smile and hurried out the door. "We're late!" she called over her shoulder.

Tony laughed and pulled himself to his feet, the last of his anxiety melting away. The crazy dame was wreaking havoc with his life. He just wished he wasn't enjoying it so much.

• • •

Jessie's eyes narrowed. "I'm not getting in that breezer," she said, her mouth puckering in a frown as she eyed the automobile in what Tony could only describe as abject horror. He couldn't keep a laugh from erupting.

"It won't hurt you, you know. And the top is up. Your hair will be fine."

"I don't care about my hair. It's the rest of me I'm worried about," Jessie said, kicking at the tire.

"I never pegged you for a wet blanket."

"I'm not!"

"Then prove it," Tony said, dangling the keys on his finger.

Jessie glared at him and snatched the keys. She stomped to the driver side of the car, though her bravado seemed to ebb the closer she got. Tony laughed and slid into the passenger side, leaning over to open her door.

"Come on."

She cautiously slid in, her eyes darting everywhere. Tony chuckled again, enjoying having the edge on her, for once. It would be fun to teach her something. Something she was afraid of.

"Put the key in here," he said, tapping the ignition. "Give it a turn."

She did as instructed, sucking in a quiet breath when the huge convertible roared to life. She gripped the steering wheel, waiting for her next instructions. If it hadn't been for the white knuckles strangling the wheel, Tony would never have guessed she was nervous. Her face was calm and collected. He couldn't help wonder what other emotions she kept buried beneath her surface. Probably as many as he did himself.

Pushing away those thoughts, he leaned over and covered her hand with his own. She glanced at him in surprise, but he kept his hand on hers until she loosened her hold a bit.

"There you go. Just relax. There's no one around," he said, gesturing to the empty lot they were in. "And as long as you stay clear of that post over there, there's nothing you can hit."

Jessie nodded and let out a long breath, turning to him with a little smile. The expression transformed her face. Excitement shone from her eyes, and though she still gripped the wheel too tightly, she didn't seem as terrified as before.

"Now. You see that pedal on the left?"

When she nodded, he continued. "You need to push that down whenever you change gears. Like this."

He took her hand and laid it on the gear stick between them, keeping his hand over hers. "Push down the pedal and keep it down until I say. Now, push the stick up," he said, guiding her hand, "and you're in first gear. Now you slowly release the left pedal while compressing the right pedal. That's your gas."

Jessie flicked a nervous glance at him but did as he directed. The car lurched forward and she shrieked, letting go of the wheel to clamp her hands over her eyes.

"Jessie!" Tony laughed and grabbed the wheel. "Give it gas. And open your eyes!" He grabbed her hand and put it back on the wheel.

Jessie quickly glanced at him, her blue eyes huge in her pale face, but he thought he caught a little twinkle of excitement as she gave the car a bit more gas and tried to ease it forward. The car lurched several times while Tony tried to direct her on how to give it just enough gas to keep it going without completely flooring the pedal.

Just when she'd get the gas figured out it would be time to shift the car and they'd have to start all over again. The poor automobile died more than once. But after a few minutes, during which Tony's lunch threatened to make a reappearance, Jessie got the hang of it and started to circle the lot—slowly.

She let out a deep breath and turned to Tony with a smile. "I'm doing it!"

He chuckled. "Yes, you are. And very well, too. Ease your grip just a bit," he said, covering her white-knuckled hand with his own.

Her eyes flicked to his but she kept her attention on the lot in front of her. Which meant Tony had the opportunity to keep his attention on her. The excitement had kept the becoming blush to her cheeks and the small smile that graced her lips softened her whole appearance. She always seemed… tired, burdened. But now, with the steering wheel in her hands and the wind gently ruffling her hair, she seemed carefree. Happy.

Tony smiled and leaned his elbow against his door, angling his body so he could more easily watch her. The warmth spreading through him at the sight of her happiness surprised him. He wasn't supposed to be making her happy. He was supposed to be pumping her for information about her alleged boyfriend's illegal activities. But he found he rather liked the feeling that came with every smile she turned his way. He'd give a great deal to see that smile on her face more often.

"What?" Jessie asked, the laugh in her voice softening the question. "Am I doing it wrong?"

Tony shook his head. "You are doing beautifully."

Jessie glanced at him, for once at a loss for words. She bit her lip and tightened her grip on the steering wheel. After that she kept her attention firmly fixed in front of her.

"Tony?"

Tony was having such a great time staring at her he didn't realize that she was in trouble until her panic raised her voice to a screech.

"Tony! What do I do?"

He finally snapped out of it and looked around, fear gripping his own gut when he saw what had scared her.

"Turn the wheel!" he yelled, jerking the wheel hard to

the right, swerving the car out of the path of an oncoming milk delivery truck. The horn of the other vehicle blared as it also swerved. They avoided hitting each other but that's where their luck ran out. When Tony had jerked the wheel, he'd aimed them right at the post at the far side of the lot and neither of them noticed they were barreling toward it until it was too late.

Jessie screamed and slammed on the brakes, throwing them both forward. The car skidded, its front end crashing into the pole. Jessie and Tony were tossed back against the seats, ending up in a jumble together.

Tony propped himself up, his heart pounding. He turned to Jessie, helping her to sit upright.

"Are you all right?"

He lightly ran his hands over her arms and torso, making sure she wasn't hurt, then traveled up to her face. He couldn't keep a chuckle from breaking out once he'd calmed down enough to get a good look at her.

Her hat had been knocked askew and hung half over her face. When he pushed it up, her eyes were as wide as the tires that were now spinning uselessly, suspended in air against the post. Her mouth hung open a bit, either in a silent scream or in response to his query. She didn't seem physically harmed, but she was certainly in complete shock.

"Jessie?"

"Huh?" She blinked at him.

"Are you all right?"

She stared blankly for another moment and then slowly nodded her head, an action which sent her hat sliding onto her face again. She snatched it off her head and tossed it to the floor of the car.

"I just…we just…" She looked out the window at the half uprooted pole. "Oh, Tony, I'm so sorry! I don't know what happened. That truck just came from nowhere. What was it doing in this lot? I thought it was abandoned. I didn't even see it until we were right on it and I just…I'm so sorry!"

Tony couldn't keep his laughter at bay this time. Jessie's contrite expression darkened into a frown at his amusement.

"I don't see what's so funny! We could have been seriously harmed and your poor car…"

"I don't care about the car," he said, leaning closer. "As long as you are fine, that's all I care about."

"I'm fine," she whispered, her blue eyes blinking up at him from under her lashes.

He reached out and brushed a lock of hair from her face, allowing his finger to trail along her cheek. The gesture instantly drew color to her cheeks and he smiled. Would that happen if he continued the path down her creamy skin?

His finger trailed down the soft skin of her neck and she froze, sucking in a breath in a little gasp. That tiny sound was all the encouragement he needed. He wrapped his hand around the back of her neck and drew her to him, his lips descending before she could protest. The moment his lips touched hers, he was lost.

She stiffened just for a second and then sank into him. Tony brought his other hand up to cup her face. He knew this was wrong. He might have taken this job, but he did have some scruples. He drew the line at physically accosting a dame just to get information.

But that wasn't what this was about anymore. Tony didn't care about Jameson, or the Phoenix, or speakeasies, or anything but the captivating woman in his arms. Her lips parted beneath his and all other thoughts vacated his mind. She nuzzled closer to him, her breasts pressing against his chest where his heart raced.

His hand moved down the column of her neck and along her shoulder, slipping into the neckline of her blouse. He pushed aside the fabric, desperate to taste the silky skin he exposed. His teeth and lips grazed her collarbone, his hand reaching between them to cup her breast. Jessie arched into him, pressing her soft flesh into his palm. His thumb brushed across the nipple that was straining through the layers she wore and Jessie moaned, sending a bolt of heat straight to Tony's core. His blood roared. He wanted her beneath him, wanted to feel her writhing against him, screaming his name.

He reached down and took the tight little bud into his mouth, gently nipping at it through the fabric.

Jessie gasped and threw her head back. "Tony!" Her hand threaded through his hair, grabbing hold of him and anchoring him in place.

Tony's trousers grew miserably tight and he wanted nothing more than to rip their clothes off and bury himself in her right then and there. He dragged her against him, his hand trailing down until he found the hem of her skirt. His fingers brushed up the length of her thigh and her fingers tightened in his hair, yanking him toward her so she could crush her lips to his.

Tony hitched her leg around his thigh, frustrated at the tight confines of the car. She whimpered and ground her hips against his. Tony groaned and deepened their kiss, his tongue delving into her sweet, moist heat.

"Tony," Jessie gasped again. "We shouldn't…"

"I know," he said, his hands following her soft curves. He grasped her firm bottom and pulled her against him, her heated softness meeting the hard, aching length of him.

Jessie threw her head back…and hit the horn on the steering wheel. The blaring sound startled a shriek out of her and Tony laughed. Jessie's cheeks turned crimson.

"I'm sorry," she muttered, extricating herself from him.

Tony chuckled again and helped her set her clothing to rights, immediately missing her warmth mingling with his. "If anyone should apologize, it should be me. Can't really bring myself to feel sorry about it, though."

Jessie looked away but Tony took her chin in his hands and gently turned her face back to him. "I've wanted to kiss you since the second I clapped eyes on you. And now that I've tasted those sweet lips of yours, there's a good deal more I'd like to do."

She shook her head and looked away. "I'm sorry...this was a mistake. I shouldn't have allowed..."

The car jolted, the bumper pulling loose from the post they rested against, and Jessie uttered another startled, "Eep!"

Tony chuckled again. "Perhaps we should inspect the damage."

Jessie nodded and turned to the door but before she could get out, Tony stopped her, capturing her face in his hands so he could press one last kiss to her delectable lips. "We'll continue this discussion later."

Before she could protest, he shoved his door open and hopped out.

Jessie pushed against her own door, which protested a bit but finally opened, allowing her to slip out. She walked to the front end, her hand over her mouth.

Tony joined her. He took off his hat and slapped it against his leg, letting out a long whistle. "Yeah, the old girl has definitely seen better days."

"Oh, very funny. You slay me."

Which only made him laugh out loud. He couldn't help himself. He reached out and grabbed her, pulling her into him for a quick kiss. She froze the moment their lips met and another bolt of heat flashed through him, turning what he'd intended to be a quick, playful peck into something much more dangerous. Another moment and he'd have her back in the car with her skirt over her head. And that was not the way he wanted their first time to be.

What the hell was he thinking? Their first time? They

couldn't be together. In any way. She was right. What had happened between them was a mistake. His feelings about this job were muddled enough. Now that he'd had a taste of her, though… He took a deep breath. Apparently, he couldn't resist making life difficult for himself.

He let go of her and she stumbled back a bit, her hand patting her hair as though putting that to rights would erase his momentary indiscretion.

"Mr. Solomon…Tony…I…that wasn't…"

"My apologies," he said, though he felt anything *but* apologetic. "I have no excuse. I just couldn't stop myself. You are just so adorable in your prim and proper suit with your hair sticking out all over your head." He ignored her gasp, laughing again when her hands flew to her hips. "You are quite fetching, Miss Harlan, standing there with your hands on your hips like a disapproving school marm."

Jessie opened her mouth to berate him, no doubt, but stopped when she looked down and saw that she was standing exactly as he'd described. Her lips twitched into a smile but she crossed her arms and turned her attention back to the car.

"So what do we do about this mess?"

"Oh, I expect the police will be along shortly. I'm sure someone has reported it by now and the coppers love to fill out their reports and issue their warnings."

"Police?" Jessie's face paled and Tony hurried to reassure her.

"No worries," he said, reaching out so he could run his hands up and down her arms in a soothing gesture he didn't realize he was doing until she stiffened and pulled away from him. For a moment he'd forgotten she had very good reason to want to avoid the police. The reminder sobered him considerably.

"We'll just tell them I was driving," he said, and she blinked up at him in surprise. "It was my fault you were driving after all. Only right I take the responsibility. Besides, if I hadn't jerked on the wheel, you probably wouldn't have hit the pole. So it really is my fault, after all."

Jessie hesitated but finally nodded. And just in time. A police car pulled up, rolling to a stop next to them. They must have purposely waited in order to make it seem like they'd needed to be summoned because Tony was well aware that there was a tail on Jessie at all hours of the day or night.

Jameson climbed out of the car, along with an officer Tony didn't know. Jessie seemed to know who he was, though. She gave the man a cool nod and ignored Jameson entirely, moving to stand closer to Tony. He hid his surprise that she seemed to want his protection, but he was more than willing to give it. He reached out to take her hand and pulled her a little behind him, not so much that it looked like he was shielding her, but enough that she wouldn't be in the officers' full line of sight.

"Well, what seems to be the trouble here," Jameson said.

Tony looked at the car resting against the post, its front tires still spinning occasionally in midair, and then back at Jameson.

"I should think that is obvious."

Jameson's eyes narrowed. "What exactly happened?"

Tony opened his mouth to give Jameson the spiel he'd made up, but Jessie spoke first.

"I wasn't aware federal officers were in charge of dealing with automobile accidents now."

"We were in the area, thought we'd stop and see if we could help."

She gave him an icy smile and for the first time Tony got a glimpse of the woman who might be mixed up with a mobster. He had a hard time reconciling this version of her with the woman he'd kissed just moments before. Before he could think too hard about it, his Jessie was back again, giving

Jameson a sheepish smile.

"Well, Agent Jameson, it's my fault entirely."

She squeezed his hand and Tony clamped his lips together to keep from berating her. It was too late to spin his story now. If he interrupted to refute her, it would just look worse.

"Would you care to elaborate, Miss Harlan?"

"Well, Mr. Solomon here had just been a lamb all morning, taking me shopping and treating me to lunch, and I'm afraid I was a little pushy about where we'd eat and Tony might have overdone it just a bit and well, when he got in the car he was feeling rather poorly so I offered to drive so he could relax. Only, I didn't mention that I didn't really know how to drive and I made a wrong turn and ended up in this old lot and then that truck over there," she said, pointing to where the truck driver had pulled over on the other side of the lot and was talking to another officer, "he pulled into the lot and I had glanced over to make sure Mr. Solomon was doing all right and I'm afraid I didn't see the truck until it was too late."

Tony and Jameson both stared at her in open-mouthed amazement. Tony, at how effortlessly, if uncharacteristically vapidly, she spun such a plausible tale to explain why their car had tried to climb a pole. Jameson was most likely struck dumb for the same reason. Though granted, Jameson was often struck dumb. It was his natural state.

Jameson finally blinked. "Is this what really happened, Solomon?"

Tony just nodded, not sure what else he could say.

Jameson snapped his notebook shut and shoved it back in his pocket. Tony fought to keep the smug and slightly disgusted look off his face. Jameson wouldn't haul them in for reckless driving. He still needed Tony to romance whatever information he could out of Jessie. And her little tale had at least helped make it look like that was exactly what Tony had been doing, though she couldn't have known it.

"Since no one else and no other property was damaged in this accident—"

"But the pole," Jessie supplied helpfully.

"But the pole," Jameson amended, glaring at her, "I see no reason to drag this out. We'll contact someone to come and tow your car."

"I'd appreciate that, thanks," Tony said, though he knew his tone was anything but thankful. Truthfully, he just wanted Jameson and his men gone.

For once, Jameson obliged. He cleared out a few minutes later. He'd offered them a ride, which they'd both turned down, so as soon as the tow truck had arrived for the car, Tony offered his arm to Jessie.

"Shall we find ourselves a cab?"

Jessie hesitated, but finally nodded and looped her arm through his. She didn't argue when he led her off down the lane. Tony kept her firmly tucked into his side and after a moment, she seemed content to stay there.

Tony was almost disappointed when they reached the main thoroughfare so he could hail a cab. He'd enjoyed their stroll, short though it had been. They hadn't spoken a word, but the silence hadn't been awkward. Tony couldn't remember a time he'd been alone with a dame who hadn't chattered his ear off. He liked just being with her. In every way.

And that thought was dangerous. He'd do well to remember who this particular woman was and what he was supposed to be doing with her.

A cab pulled up and Tony opened the door for Jessie, sliding in after her. He gave the driver the address to Jessie's shop and settled back against the seat. Jessie held herself stiffly on her side, her back barely touching the leather. Tony ran a finger down her arm and her gaze shot to him in surprise.

"That was quick thinking back there."

Her eyes narrowed for a moment and then relaxed in

understanding. "I saw the other officer talking to the truck driver. He probably saw me behind the wheel. If you'd said you were driving, they would have known you were lying."

"I'm impressed. I didn't even notice the other officer."

Jessie shrugged. "I've found it useful to be observant."

"Why is that?"

Jessie looked out the window, not answering him. Tony didn't want to push but he needed her to start opening up about the Phoenix. The sooner he found out who the man was, the sooner the Feds could get him out of Jessie's life. And then she'd be free.

"Has your singing in my club caused any problems for you?"

Jessie turned to him, her brow creased. "What do you mean?"

Surely she wouldn't make him spell it out.

Jessie continued to wait in silence for his answer and he held back an exasperated sigh.

"I mean is there anyone who disapproves of you working for me? I wouldn't want to cause you any trouble."

She shrugged and looked back out her window. "I'm my own woman. I can do as I like, regardless of who it upsets."

He'd take that as a yes. The Phoenix must not like his woman working for the competition. Not surprising. But Tony didn't want to place Jessie in danger. "It must upset your man to have you in my club."

A faint smile creased Jessie's lips. "I am exactly where the Phoenix wants me."

Tony's eyebrows rose at that. She'd never referred to the Phoenix directly before.

She saw his expression and laughed. "I'll never understand why men always underestimate women. I'm fully aware of why you want me singing in your club, Tony. You want information on the Phoenix. Well, the Phoenix wants information on you, too. What better way to scope out the competition than to have someone on the inside?"

Tony sat back against the seat, trying to keep his face from showing his inner turmoil. She was playing both sides. Clever little minx. But why was she telling him? He leaned away from her a bit so he could better watch her. "And what exactly have you told him?"

"All the Phoenix knows is that you serve watered down whiskey and have a phenomenal singer for entertainment."

Tony watched her closely, not sure if she was being honest or not. Was she trying to protect him? He couldn't figure her out. She dallied with mobsters, but seemed so innocent. She had every reason to mistrust him yet she was admitting she'd been sent by the Phoenix.

Then again, he didn't see how she *could* know anything else about him. She obviously didn't know he was working for the Feds or she wouldn't be sitting beside him. Nor would she have allowed him to take such liberties. Just the thought of that kiss had him fighting the urge to haul her against him and finish what he'd started. But that course of action seemed even more unwise in light of what she'd just told him. His little Miss Harlan wasn't exactly as she seemed.

Still, he didn't like that she was in the middle of all this. She shouldn't be the pawn in a game she had no business being in. And playing both sides was a good way to double her chances of getting hurt.

"He can't be happy if that's all you've told him."

Jessie shrugged again. "That's all I know. Why do you care if the Phoenix is happy or not?"

Tony stared at her, unsure of how to answer. He wasn't sure himself why he cared so much. But he did.

He reached out and cupped her cheek in his hand. "I don't want you in danger."

For a sweet moment, she closed her eyes and leaned her

face against his palm. His heart clenched at the sight. And when she turned slightly so her lips barely brushed against his skin, he wanted nothing more than to bury his fingers in her hair and pull her to him so he could taste that sweet mouth.

"There's no help for that now," she said quietly, drawing away from him.

She was right. She'd made her bed, as they say, and now she'd have to live with the consequences. She couldn't associate with criminals and expect to come away unscathed.

But for the first time, Tony wished that circumstances were different. That he could somehow get the information he needed without using her. Find a way to get her out of the whole mess. Away from the Phoenix *and* the Feds. Before it was too late.

Chapter Eleven

Jessie threw herself face down on her bed and groaned into her pillow. Maude perched on the end of the mattress, filing her nails. She waited until Jessie came up for air before she zinged her with, "I told you so."

Jessie glared at her. "That's incredibly unhelpful."

Maude shrugged. "That's all I've got for you, ducky. I'm not sure what you expected to happen."

"Well I didn't expect that I'd...that he'd...that I..."

Maude laughed. "That you'd like him?"

Jessie did another face dive into her pillows. When she flipped onto her back, Maude was still patiently filing her nails and watching her.

"I don't like him," Jessie said.

Maude snorted.

"I don't!"

"Then what is all this about?" Maude asked, waving at Jessie with her nail file. "Women do not act like this over men who mean nothing to them. Mind you, I don't blame you one bit. He is the absolute cat's meow. If I'd have seen him first, I'd have abandoned you and The Red Phoenix and hightailed it over to The Corkscrew the first chance I got."

Jessie ignored her, knowing her friend didn't mean it. Or only half meant it, anyway. Maude loved handsome men and wasn't shy about who knew it. And Tony was definitely handsome.

Jessie flung her arm over her eyes. "You know he only wants me in his club so he can get information on the Phoenix."

Maude shrugged. "You only took the job because you wanted information on him. Fair's fair, I say."

Jessie knew she had no right to be mad at Tony for doing what she was doing herself, but still, it stung to think he might only be interested in her for what she knew about the Phoenix.

"What is it?" Maude pressed again.

"I don't know," Jessie sighed.

"He's not Mario, doll. You can't judge every man by that piece of filth."

Jessie jerked up at the mention of her ex's name. "I know that. And I'm not, I swear. But…It's just…it doesn't seem like that's all he wants. I mean, he does ask me about the Phoenix, but sometimes, I swear that…that he…"

"That he might be interested in you for more than who you are in bed with?"

Jessie's mouth dropped open. "I am not in bed with the Phoenix." She didn't even pause to think about how ridiculous that statement was.

Maude cocked an eyebrow. "Oh, stop splitting hairs. What's the hotsy-totsy Mr. Solomon doing that makes you think he's more than a little interested in you?"

Jessie plucked at a loose thread on her dress, not meeting her friend's eyes. "I'm sure I'm just reading things into it."

Maude abandoned her nail file and lounged against the headboard, tucking her manicured feet under her. "You just let me be the judge of that," she said, pulling Jessie's arm off her eyes. "Now, tell me everything."

Jessie shrugged. "It's nothing really. Just...the way he looks at me sometimes."

"Yes..." Maude prompted with a gleam in her eye.

"And the other day, after our little accident, when we were in the cab. He held my face," she said, her hand mimicking the way Tony's hand had cradled her cheek, "and he said that he didn't want me to be in danger."

"Oh, honey, that man is definitely interested in you."

"Well, yes, but how do I know if it's me that he wants or if he's just..."

"Trying to romance some information out of you?"

"Yes."

"I guess you'll just have to trust your instincts."

Jessie snorted. "Because that worked so well for me before."

Maude frowned at her. "You aren't the same person you were back then. And I'll bet if you are really honest with yourself, you knew something was fishy with Mario. You just ignored your gut. So this time, don't ignore it."

Jessie sighed. "Easier said than done. Just when I think I've got a handle on everything, something happens that throws me completely off balance."

"Something happens?" Maude said, perking up. "Like what, exactly?"

Jessie mentally kicked herself for mentioning it.

"Jessica Harlan, you'd better start flappin' those lips right now and tell me what happened!"

"He kissed me," she said, and then slapped her hands over her face.

Maude crowed and clapped her hands. "Why didn't you say so sooner? He kissed you? Oh how delicious, tell me *everything*!"

"It was nothing."

Maude snorted. "It was more than nothing, or your cheeks wouldn't be hot enough to light my ciggy. Just what exactly happened?"

Jessie slapped her hands over her cursed cheeks. "He must think I'm nothing but some two-timin' floozy."

"Oh, honey. I'm sure you're wrong."

"But he thinks I'm the Phoenix's girl, but we…I mean I let him…"

"You let him what?" Maude asked, her bright eyes round in anticipation.

Jessie rolled her eyes. "Never you mind. Doesn't matter anyhow, I guess. It didn't get too far. I hit the horn and startled some sense into us, and then Jameson came…"

Maude wrinkled her nose and waved off that comment. "Then what?"

"Then nothing."

"*Hmm*. Well. How was it?"

"How was what?"

"The kiss. Or whatever else you did," she said with a wink. "Was it nice? Did you like it?"

"Oh." Jessie bit her lip to keep from smiling. "It was… you know…"

"Oh, yes, I *do* know." Maude sighed and slumped farther down on the pillows.

Jessie just flipped over and buried her face in her pillow.

"That good, huh?" Maude laughed, her low, husky laugh that made men drool at her feet. "I bet it was."

"Oh, Maude," Jessie said, slapping her friend's arm. "What do I do now?"

"If it were me, I'd march right back into that man's office and kiss him until he couldn't even look at another woman but me."

Jessie frowned. She'd love to do that. In fact, every cell in her body fairly screamed to do it. But it was never going to happen.

"But you aren't me," Maude said with a sigh. "What do you want to do?"

"I really don't know. I know I can't trust him. I know he only wants to seduce me to get information out of me. And I don't know what his connection to Jameson is yet. They obviously aren't friends, but they know each other and that is concerning. So to get involved with him would be foolish. Especially since he's also my competition."

"So. You have a lot of reasons to stay away from him."

"Yes."

"But?"

Jessie shrugged. "There is no *but*. It's foolish. It doesn't matter what I might want—"

"So you *do* want to be with him! I knew it."

The ridiculous butterflies that had erupted in her belly at the memory of the kiss faded away with the cold light of reality. "I don't know what I want."

"I think you do," Maude said gently, reaching over to brush Jessie's hair out of her face. "Now you just need to find out how to go about getting it."

"It's not that easy."

"You are making this too complicated."

"No, I'm not. It's plenty complicated without any help from me."

Maude shook her head. "You are both over thinking this. You want him. He wants you. Nothing else should matter."

Jessie leaned against her friend's shoulder, wishing it really was that simple. Unfortunately, other things did matter. Far too much.

· · ·

Tony sat across from Jameson at the diner, his coffee growing cold in front of him, trying his hardest to hold his patience. The man had been quizzing him for more than an hour now while he shoved his breakfast down his throat, and Tony had no more information to pass along than he had when they'd started. Finally, he held up a hand.

Jameson stopped eating and frowned at him. "What?"

"Agent Jameson, I can appreciate your situation. I know you want the Phoenix. I am doing my best to get you the information you need. But I won't be able to do that from this diner and me being seen with you won't do anything but blow my cover."

Jameson waved him off. "The bootleggers would be more suspicious if we weren't harassing you and pulling you in for questioning every other day. They'd wonder why we were leaving you alone."

"Be that as it may, I can't do the job you hired me for in here."

"Doesn't seem like you are doing the job you were hired for out there, either."

Tony glared at him, angry that there was more than a little truth to that. Jameson exhaled and leaned back, crossing his hands over his stomach. "Fine."

Tony stood to go but Jameson stopped him. "Just a minute. There's one other matter we need to discuss."

Tony sat back down and linked his fingers over his chest, waiting for Jameson to get to the point. Jameson pulled a piece of paper from his pocket and tossed it in front of him. Tony glanced at it but didn't pick it up.

"Care to explain why you spent almost $100 on a bunch of dresses?"

Tony kept his amusement to himself. He'd wondered when Jameson would bring it up. "I thought I was free to use the money at my disposal as I saw fit."

Jameson's eyes narrowed dangerously. "To a point. That

money is only to be used to maintain your cover, to keep the speakeasy running."

"I hired a new singer for the club. She needed something to wear."

Jameson's eyebrow twitched. "That's quite a few somethings."

"If my club is going to be popular enough to rival The Red Phoenix, then we need to step up our game. We'll never draw the Phoenix out unless we make this look realistic."

Jameson downed the rest of his coffee, his patience for the subject obviously at an end. Tony stood to go but Jameson's voice stopped him again.

"Wait. Who is this singer you've hired?"

Tony inwardly swore. He'd been hoping he wouldn't have to divulge Jessie's identity just yet. He turned around, braced himself for Jameson's explosion, and said, "Jessica Harlan."

"Excuse me?"

Tony didn't repeat himself. Jameson had heard.

Jameson threw a few bills on the table and stood. "Well, that's one way of keeping her close to you. That's one hell of a large development and a definite stride in the right direction. You didn't think it important enough to mention to me?"

Jameson's voice was low, controlled, but that didn't fool Tony. The man was probably two seconds away from popping a few holes in him. And understandably so. But Tony had his reasons for wanting to keep Jessie a secret. Reasons he didn't intend to share with Jameson.

"I didn't want to say anything until I had something concrete to tell you. She's only just started and I haven't been able to gather any information from her yet. I'm not so sure she knows anything at all. She works all day in that butcher shop, and from what I can gather, she rarely ventures out at night. If she's still the Phoenix's broad, which I'm beginning to doubt, then they are awfully secretive about meeting."

Jameson scowled. "Don't let that sweet little face of hers distract you, Solomon. She knows a lot more than she's letting on. And if she's agreed to work for you it can only be so she can spy on you for him. Did that ever occur to you?"

Tony glared at Jameson in disgust. "Of course it did. You might not be happy with my methods at the moment, but I know what I'm doing."

"Really? And what is it that you are doing, aside from letting the enemy in your front door?"

"We haven't been able to draw the Phoenix out with the club's success alone but he should be poking around by now. The Corkscrew is making a nice little dent in his bottom line, but until Jessie agreed to work at my club, there hadn't been one incident that pointed to the Phoenix caring a whit for me stealing his clientele. Now that I've got Jessie, maybe we can draw him out a little faster."

Jameson studied Tony for a moment, then finally sat back in his chair with a slow smile. "Excellent. Very smart. If he doesn't care about you stealing his business, or his girlfriend getting romanced out from under him, maybe he'll care if she leaves his team to work for yours. Well done. Well, far be it from me to get in your way. Carry on, Solomon."

Tony turned and stalked out, his gut turning at the admiration in Jameson's voice. He also shoved away the twinge of unease that crept in every time he thought of the information he did know that he wasn't sharing. Such as the fact that the nights Jessie wasn't at The Corkscrew were very likely the nights The Red Phoenix was up and running. Really, Jameson should have known enough to ask about that on his own. How the man had made it into the Bureau was beyond Tony. And Tony would tell him…soon.

He blew out a breath and picked up his pace, ignoring his surroundings and the people he brushed past in his hurry. In the beginning, this had all seemed like a good idea. But now…

the thought of using her to get to her rum running boyfriend sat like a bad egg in the pit of his stomach. She obviously knew more about the Phoenix's business than she wanted to let on. She'd be useful, even instrumental, in taking down the Phoenix. But while Tony knew it was the best way, the whole plan still stuck in his craw.

Especially now that things between them had escalated. He'd never intended to lay a hand on her, let alone his lips or...anything else. He might use a little romance to get what he needed every now and then, but he drew the line at seducing a girl. If he had any smarts, he'd get out now before things got worse.

No help for it now, though, and he had no choice. He'd started on this path and he would have to see it through. He just needed to make sure nothing like that little scene in the car ever happened again. Jessie was off-limits, end of story. Tony sucked in a deep breath, trying to ease the sudden tightness in his chest. The thought of never touching Jessie again, of doing his job and walking away forever, bothered him more than it should. What the hell had he gotten himself into?

Maybe a reminder of why he was doing this would make everything more palatable. He doubted it, but it was worth a shot.

Chapter Twelve

Jessie watched Tony leave the diner, followed only seconds later by Jameson. The man was an idiot. If he had any intention of keeping his connection to Tony a secret, he'd just blown it. Though the arrogant stooge probably didn't care.

Then again, Tony wouldn't be the first bootlegger the agent had invited to a civilized lunch so they could discuss "business." It gave him the chance to let the enemy know he was keeping an eye on things, do a little light interrogating in a non-threatening environment, while allowing him to charge a free lunch to the Feds' bill. Jessie had been invited to just such a lunch in the not-too-distant past. It didn't necessarily mean Tony was on Jameson's side.

But it didn't look good.

Jessie took a deep breath past the lump in her throat. She was taking this too personally. She'd suspected Tony was in cahoots with Jameson, had known Tony was only interested in her for her connection to the Phoenix. Still, thinking you knew something and being confronted with proof were two entirely different things. Especially in light of her growing feelings for him. Feelings that she needed to bump off before she got in way over her head.

"Where are you going now, you little rat fink?" she muttered to herself, her eyes narrowing as Tony hurried across the road to her side of the street.

She hadn't meant to follow him. She'd been out running a few errands when she'd seen him huddled over a cuppa joe with that sniveling excuse for a man, Jameson. And the sight had hurt far more than she'd expected. He certainly seemed like he was in a rush now. Jessie set off after him before she made the conscious decision to do so.

She followed him several blocks, the shops and apartment buildings getting more dilapidated as they went, until finally he turned down an alley between two of the tenements. She slowed up as she reached the corner, peeking around cautiously to see where he'd gone.

Tony was leaning over to kiss the head of an old woman who was sitting on a chair outside her stoop. About ten feet away. Jessie ducked back around the corner, but the old woman had spotted her, for sure. Maybe she wouldn't say anything. Jessie turned to hurry off, just in case.

No such luck.

"Jessie?" Tony's curious and highly displeased voice stopped her in her tracks.

She turned back around, head held high. He was the one who had some explaining to do. She was not going to apologize.

"What are you doing here?" he asked.

"I'm sorry, I just…" She sighed. So much for not apologizing. Well, no point in trying to lie her way out of this one, even if she could. Evading, she could do. Lying, she wasn't so good at.

"I was just running some errands and saw you…"

Tony's eyebrow popped up, his face hardening, though

the expression looked more defensive than accusatory.

"I saw you walking this way and thought I'd say hi."

His face relaxed a bit. "Why didn't you call out?"

The better question was why didn't she admit she'd seen him with Jameson? She wasn't sure herself. "Well, I wasn't sure it was you, so…"

"Anthony? Who is your friend?"

Jessie peeked around Tony's barrel of a chest. The old woman stood at the corner of the building, leaning on a cane, her white hair pulled back in a bun that was doing a lousy job of keeping her hair in order.

"Ma," Tony said, immediately turning to take her arm, "you'll tire yourself out. Go back and sit down." He began to lead her back to her stoop but she pulled back to look at Jessie.

"Why don't you bring your lady friend?"

Tony looked at Jessie almost helplessly and Jessie couldn't help but smile. "Thank you, Mrs. Solomon."

Tony shot her an exasperated look but didn't protest when she followed him back down the clothesline strewn alleyway to his mother's stoop.

"Let's go inside, Anthony. It'll be much more comfortable for a little visit."

Tony had a pained look on his face, but again he didn't argue, just obeyed without comment. It was all Jessie could do to keep her amazement to herself. Her arrogant, bootlegging boss had turned into an obedient, albeit reluctant, mama's boy.

Tony helped his mother up the steps that led into the building and into the first apartment just inside the door. Jessie followed them into a sparse but well-kept apartment.

"Please, sit down, deary," Mrs. Solomon said, pointing at a threadbare armchair set up opposite an equally ragged sofa.

"How about a nice cup of tea?"

"Oh, I don't want to be any trouble."

"Nonsense! Anthony will get us all set up. He's quite handy in the kitchen."

"He is, *hmm*?" Jessie smiled and Tony glared at her. Which only made Jessie smile wider. She just could not picture this man aproned up and running amuck in a kitchen.

"Ma, I don't think—"

"Oh hush. Go on now and let me get acquainted with your friend."

Tony headed to the kitchen, giving Jessie what she assumed was a warning glare as he passed her. Only what he was warning against, she had no idea.

"Now, what is your name, my dear?"

"Oh, I'm so sorry. I'm Jessica Harlan. I'm very pleased to meet you."

"Miss Harlan. And how do you know my Anthony?"

"I um, well…"

Jessie had no idea what this woman might or might not know about her son's activities. She certainly didn't want to be the one to spoil any family secrets.

Luckily, Tony piped up from the small kitchen where he was putting the kettle on. "I met Jessie in her butcher shop a few weeks ago."

"Oh, you're a butcher? How interesting."

Jessie smiled politely.

"She's also just started singing in my club, though that took a little convincing."

Jessie's gaze shot to Tony's, her mouth open in surprise. So, apparently his mother knew everything about her son.

"Ah, so you're the one?"

"Pardon?"

"Ma," Tony said in a warning tone.

"Oh, Anthony, why don't you grab us a few cookies out of that new tin you brought me the other day." She leaned forward and patted Jessie's hand. "Anthony always brings me the yummiest treats. He's such a good boy."

Good boy wasn't really how Jessie would describe him, but he did seem to be a wonderful son. In fact, watching him putter in his mother's kitchen, carefully handing her a cup of tea with her favorite cookies, was making Jessie all warm and gooey inside. A feeling she wanted to rip out and strangle before it took hold. She could not afford to see this man as anything other than the information-digging bootlegger that he was. Hard to do when his sweet, white-haired mother was gazing at him adoringly.

"They look delicious," Jessie said, since his mother seemed to be waiting for her to say something.

Mrs. Solomon nodded. "He serves them at his club. Brings me home the extras," she said with a smile.

"That's very kind of him."

"It's a definite perk. But then he was always fond of his sweets. Even as a little boy. Couldn't keep him away from the stuff. He had the cutest chubby cheeks…"

"Ma!"

"Well, you did," she insisted.

Jessie put her hand over her mouth to hide her laughter. Tony just shook his head, though Jessie didn't miss the smile he gave his mother before he turned back to the kitchen. Jessie could barely keep an *Awww* from escaping. It was too sweet for words.

She'd once had someone tell her that you could tell how a man would treat you by how he treated his mother. Good advice—and some she wished she'd taken before she'd gotten involved with Mario Russo, that was for sure. The man had ripped her heart out even before he'd betrayed her to Willie. Maybe if she'd seen him with his mother she'd have had a clue about his true nature before she'd gotten in too deep.

If that advice was sound, though, perhaps Tony Solomon wasn't so bad after all, no matter who he might be mixed up with. Surely any man who could be so gentle and kind to his mother was decent.

"So." Mrs. Solomon settled back in her chair with a sigh. "You're a butcher. That's a bit unusual for a woman."

"I suppose," Jessie said. "My father ran the shop, and when he died I took over."

"Oh, I'm sorry to hear that. Has he been gone long?"

"Two years."

"And your mother?"

Tony came in from the kitchen, wiping his hands on a towel, and sat down on the couch beside his mother. He grabbed a handful of cookies and settled back, waiting for her answer.

Jessie squirmed. They hadn't ever spoken of personal things. Nothing real. They danced around the real issues each was trying to find out about the other, flirted a little. More than a little. But most of that wasn't genuine. Except maybe that episode in the car...it had been fast, spur of the moment, but surely the heat and emotion that had been palpable behind it hadn't been faked.

She looked away from him, trying to keep her damn cheeks from betraying her feelings yet again.

Mrs. Solomon was waiting for her answer.

"My mother's been gone since I was little."

"Oh, my dear, that's such a shame. She must have been young when she died."

Jessie shifted on her chair and put her cookie back on her saucer. "She didn't die. She just left."

The sudden silence in the room made Jessie look up. Mrs. Solomon looked as though she were trying to come up with something to say. Tony was staring at her with an intensity that made her squirm.

"It's all right," she assured them. "Dad and I did fine together. I helped him run the shop and he taught me everything I needed to know. We took care of each other."

Mrs. Solomon reached over and patted her on the knee. "You're a strong one. Got a good head on your shoulders. I like you," she declared, settling back against her cushions again.

Jessie couldn't help but smile at her.

"And now you are singing in Anthony's club."

"Ma," Tony said.

"Oh, you hush. You never tell me anything fun. What's it like getting all dolled up and singing onstage, Jessie? I always wanted to be in one of those vaudeville shows. Is it like that?"

Jessie laughed and answered as many of Mrs. Solomon's questions as she could. When Tony finally stood and said it was time that they left, Jessie was surprised to find an hour had passed.

"Thank you for the tea, Mrs. Solomon. I enjoyed meeting you."

"Oh, it was my pleasure, my dear. You come and visit me again, you hear?"

Jessie smiled shyly. "I'd love to."

"And you, bring me more cookies next time you come. You've about cleaned me out again."

She swatted her son on his arm, but he laughed and leaned down to kiss her cheek. "I'll see you later, Ma."

Mrs. Solomon waved them off. Once they were outside, Tony offered Jessie his arm and she didn't hesitate before taking it. She didn't know his reasons for meeting with Jameson, and she knew she'd be a fool to trust him completely, but she just couldn't believe that a man who loved his mother the way Tony obviously did was that bad.

"I'm sorry about all that," Tony said. "My mother can be a bit…eccentric."

"And how."

Tony laughed.

"Honestly, though, I enjoyed myself."

"I'm glad," Tony said, smiling down at her. He pulled her a little closer and steered her down the sidewalk back toward the diner.

They walked in companionable silence for a few minutes and Jessie found herself wishing they were two normal people. Just a normal couple, maybe going on their first date. No speakeasies, no Agent Jamesons between them. Just Jessie and Tony.

Unfortunately, wishing wouldn't make all the obstacles between them disappear.

When they got to the diner, Tony paused. "Are you hungry? We could stop in, get a bite to eat."

Jessie hesitated. She wanted to say yes. What could a little dinner hurt? A girl had to eat.

But instead, she looked up into those deep brown eyes of his and pulled away. "I umm...I'd better be getting back to the shop. Joe will be wanting to close up soon."

Tony's lips pressed together, but he nodded. "Sure. I understand."

He stepped out to the curb and waved his arm to flag down a cab. When one pulled up, he opened the back door for her and held out a hand to help her inside.

"I enjoyed spending the afternoon with you, Jessie."

"I enjoyed it too," she said quietly. She let him hold her hand as she slid into the cab. When he didn't relinquish it, she looked up at him.

"I'll see you tomorrow night then."

Jessie nodded, holding her breath when he brought her hand to his lips. "Have a pleasant evening, Jessie."

"You too, Tony."

He nodded at her, eyes locked, until the cab pulled off.

Jessie leaned her head back against the seat and kicked herself for not saying yes to dinner. She knew it was the smart thing to do, but sometimes playing it smart was a real drag.

Chapter Thirteen

Tony had done his best to stay away from Jessie in the days following her visit to his mother's. Not that it was easy, watching her sing in his club. And his mother was no help either. She'd taken a shine to Jessie. Her response to his explanation of who Jessie was and why he was involved with her was a roll of the eyes. "Oh posh," she'd said. "That girl is as much of a criminal as I am. Besides, she's too far gone on you for her to be involved with anyone else."

Tony wasn't sure what to believe. He'd always trusted his mother's instincts. She'd hated Lucille. Had never trusted her and had known her feelings for Tony hadn't been genuine. And she'd been right. Maybe she was right about Jessie, as well.

Well, whether she was or wasn't, he was getting nowhere with his investigation. It was time to get down to business.

When he pulled up to the butcher shop, the sign on the door said CLOSED. He tried the knob anyway. It wasn't locked so he went ahead and entered.

"Jessie?"

No answer. There didn't seem to be anyone around, though the lights were all on. It was early yet, but still, by that time of the morning the shop should have been open for business.

"Jessie?" he called again, beginning to be a bit concerned.

"Tony? Is that you?"

Her voice was muffled. He walked through the doors leading into the back room and saw the big cellar doors open.

"Jessie?"

"Down here."

Tony peered down the steps and removed his jacket, laying it over a chair near the doors before he went down. He found her in the giant refrigerator, hacking away at a hunk of meat.

"Hey," Jessie said, smiling up at him.

"What is all this?" Tony gestured to the piles of meat spread all around her.

"It's the first of the month."

"So you decided to come down here and carve up a whole herd of cattle?"

Jessie laughed and Tony realized that he'd never heard her laugh before. A few chuckles here and there, but not this full-bellied, carefree laughter. The sound of it warmed its way through him like a sunbeam breaking through the clouds. He liked the sound of it, liked the way her face lit up, how her eyes shone like two bright little sapphires. He smiled back at her.

"No," she said, still laughing. "No, the first of every month I bring meat down to the orphanage. It takes a while to carve up, though. I usually do it the night before, but I was singing at your club last night so I didn't have time to get it all done."

"So you closed your shop on a Saturday?"

Jessie shrugged and wiped an arm across her brow before slinging another slab of meat onto her butcher block. "No helping it. Charlie is out making deliveries all day. We'll lose some profits, but it's just one day. And the children need the meat. They don't always get much in the way of fresh meat and produce."

Tony stared at her, once again surprised. Whatever her reasons for being mixed up with the likes of the Phoenix, he didn't think it had anything to do with money. Saturdays were probably her busiest days. She stood to lose a lot by closing it down, yet it didn't seem to bother her. Either she had enough in the bank that losing a whole day of profits just didn't matter…or she really didn't care.

"Could you bring me that tray over there?" she asked.

He grabbed the one she'd indicated and set it beside her on the block. She started stacking the cuts on the tray.

"You do this every month?"

"Yes. I try to get out there twice a month, if I can. Even with refrigeration, the meat will spoil if I bring too much at once."

"How long have you been doing this?"

Jessie shrugged. "For as long as I can remember. My father started the tradition."

"And you've kept it going now that he's gone."

Jessie shifted, still talking but her easygoing manner had disappeared.

"The children need it. And it's the least I can do. It's how we met."

A faint smile touched her lips and Tony's heart stopped, pieces starting to fall into place. "You lived at the orphanage?"

Jessie paused and took a deep breath. "Yes." She looked up at him, meeting his gaze, that small smile trembling on her lips. "My mother left me there when I was six years old."

"Jessie…" he said, his heart twisting at the thought of what she'd been through.

She shrugged and went back to carving. "My dad found

me, adopted me. And I couldn't have asked for a better father." Her voice cracked on the last word and she cleared her throat. "Anyway, Joe usually helps me but he's not feeling very well today."

"So you're down here all alone."

"There isn't anyone else." She slapped another steak on the pile.

Tony wanted to ask where the Phoenix was, why the man she was risking everything for couldn't lend her a hand. But he supposed a man like the Phoenix wouldn't bother spending his time on manual labor. If there even was a Phoenix.

The thought had been niggling at him. Jessie never mentioned him, never acted as though she had a lover who might have a care for her thoughts or actions. No one had ever seen him. Or at least the Feds hadn't found anyone willing to admit ever seeing him. The man was a ghost. Which didn't necessarily mean he wasn't real. Plenty of criminals were good at covering their tracks and staying out of the limelight.

But if there wasn't a Phoenix, then who was running the operation? Who was really behind The Red Phoenix? It couldn't be Willie…he was too interested in the Phoenix himself for him to already be involved with it. So who was it?

Tony took a closer look at Jessie, for the first time wondering if *she* was behind it all. It was unthinkable, unbelievable. Not impossible. But still…

"Besides, I don't mind. It gives me a chance to relax," Jessie said, breaking into his thoughts.

Tony laughed. "This is your idea of relaxing?"

Jessie smiled up at him and the ache in his heart eased a little. "It's repetitive, doesn't require a lot of thought. It's quiet down here. And I enjoy the work."

She brought the knife down with a thwack.

"I can see that." Tony watched her carefully. She was handy with that knife. Yes, she was referencing it in terms of her job. But she could probably be very lethal, if she chose to be.

"Well," he said, pushing those thoughts aside. He had no proof Jessie was a bootlegger, or a rumrunner, and if she was, she wasn't doing it on her own, and she certainly wasn't some knife-wielding crazy. He grabbed an apron off a hook by the door and draped it over his neck. "What can I do to help?"

"You don't have to—"

"I want to. So, what can I do?"

Jessie stared at him for a second and then smiled. "These all need to be wrapped. There's a roll of paper behind you there."

He nodded and got to work.

They worked together for a few hours, sometimes chitchatting, sometimes working in silence. She'd been right. It was relaxing. The cellar shut out all sounds of the outside world. It felt like there was no one for miles but just the two of them. All his cares slipped from his mind.

He watched her. She was such a mystery. A poor little orphan girl who'd been rescued by a lonely butcher and who'd grown up to be…what? A gangster's girlfriend? A rumrunner or bootlegger in her own right? Or a simple butcher who donated her time, money, and talents to the orphanage that had taken her in? Could she be all three?

When they'd finally finished, Jessie leaned against the butcher block with a tired sigh. She glanced at the stacks of wrapped meat and turned a weary smile to Tony.

"Thank you for your help."

He pulled the apron off over his head, leaning in close to her as he laid it across the butcher block. "It was my pleasure."

She looked up at him through her dark lashes. "I'm sure you had a hundred other things to do today."

He shook his head, pleased that she didn't back away. "There is nowhere else I want to be."

She licked her bottom lip and it was all Tony could do to keep from pulling her to him and following suit.

"Well, then. Charlie should be back any minute with the truck. Would you like to come with me to make the delivery?"

"I'm yours for as long as you need me," he said, surprised that he meant every word.

She blinked up at him, her lips slightly parted, and he couldn't resist anymore. He reached out, cupping her face, drawing his thumb along her lower lip, following the path her tongue had just taken. She tilted her face up, her breath coming in short little bursts that had his heart hammering out of his chest. He stepped closer, leaned down…

"Miss Jessie?" a young man's voice called from upstairs.

Jessie jumped back out of Tony's reach, her eyes as wide as tumbler glasses. "Down here, Charlie!"

Tony grudgingly backed away, inwardly cursing the kid. Charlie thundered down the stairs, coming to an abrupt halt when he saw Tony leaning against the wall.

"Did you need something, Charlie?"

The youth tore his eyes away from Tony and nodded at Jessie. "Yes, ma'am. The truck is all ready for you."

"Oh wonderful, Charlie. You're an absolute angel."

Charlie blushed a deep crimson and Tony's eyes narrowed. Charlie caught sight of his expression and backed up a step.

"I'll, um…I'll just start loading these up," he said, grabbing a box of the meat Tony had wrapped.

"Thanks, Charlie. We're right behind you."

Tony didn't take his eyes off the boy until he'd disappeared back up the stairs. Jessie walked over and slapped his arm.

"Ow," he said, chuckling. "What was that for?"

"You! Glaring at poor Charlie! What's wrong with you?"

Tony wrapped an arm around her waist and drew her closer to him, inhaling her sweet jasmine sent. "I didn't like the way he was looking at you."

Jessie sputtered a bit, halfheartedly struggling against him, and he closed his eyes with a groan, pressing her closer. If she didn't hold still, he'd lock them in and Charlie could be damned. She tried to frown at him but she couldn't keep a smile from peeking through. "He's just a kid. He's harmless."

"He's not much younger than you, I'd bet, and I remember myself at that age. Trust me, he's not harmless."

Jessie laughed and the sound hit Tony right in the heart. Damn, but the woman was doing a number on him. Who was romancing who here?

"Come on, he's going to be wondering what's taking us so long."

She reached up on her tiptoes and planted a kiss on his cheek. She tried to spin away but Tony kept his arm around her and pulled her back into his chest.

"Let him wonder," he said, his other hand trailing up to cup her face.

She leaned into him and Tony brushed his lips across hers, lightly tasting. She rose on her toes again, deepening the kiss before he had a chance to. He wrapped his arms around her waist and lifted her off the ground, leaning back slightly so the full weight of her body rested against his.

A banging from upstairs announced Charlie's imminent return and they reluctantly came up for air. Jessie pushed away from him, her hand going quickly to her hair. Then she smiled up at him, grabbed him by the lapels and pulled him down for another quick kiss, letting him go just as Charlie stomped down the stairs.

Tony laughed, wishing he could kick the door closed and finish what she'd seemed very willing to start. Two problems with that idea, though. One, they were in a refrigerator surrounded by meat and there were warmer, and more romantic, locations he'd prefer to be. And two, the ever-helpful Charlie would spoil the mood for sure.

Jessie hefted a box and thrust it into Tony's hands. He held on, pulling her forward for one last kiss, but she grinned and pushed him away. "Sorry, baby, but this bank's closed. Now go load the truck."

She spun away with a wink and Tony chuckled. Hot damn, but he'd love to get her good and alone for longer than five minutes.

He helped Charlie load up the rest of the truck and then sent the kid ahead of them. He could drive Jessie in his car. Charlie sullenly drove off and Tony went back inside to find Jessie.

She wasn't in the refrigerator, nor anywhere else in the cellar.

"Jessie?"

"I'll be up in a moment."

He looked around, trying to see where her voice had come from. In a far corner, a trapdoor had been lifted and a flickering light shone from below. Tony peered down inside, then slowly descended the stone steps until he came to a short hallway. The light was coming from a doorway on the right. The sound of glass bottles clanking together came from inside and he followed the noise.

He stopped short. Several rows of shelves held what must have been a hundred bottles of homemade gin.

"Jessie?"

She turned, barely glancing at him before placing another bottle in the satchel she held. She slung it over her shoulder and waited, watching him.

He realized she was waiting for some reaction, waiting to see what he'd do, what he'd say. He looked around, honestly not sure what to make of it. Tony's chest tightened, excitement spiking through him, and he tried to school his face, to let nothing that he was feeling show. Had she just led him right to the Phoenix's cache of booze? And if she had, why? What did it mean? What did she want him to do?

Tony thought furiously. He needed to be smart about this. One false move and every moment he'd spent building their relationship would come crashing down around him, ruining his chances of catching the big fish. Even as the thought ran through his mind, Tony knew that wasn't the real reason he wanted to handle this right.

He messed this up and he'd lose her. And he didn't want that, plain and simple.

He stepped farther into the room, ran a finger along a row of bottles.

"This is quite a stash," he said. Jessie nodded stiffly, but didn't say anything.

It was an impressive collection. But not enough to run an operation like The Red Phoenix. Not for long, anyway. So either this was Jessie's private stores or it was only the tip of the iceberg.

Finally, he sighed. He was tired of the games. "Why did you want me to see this?"

She blinked, apparently surprised at his bluntness. But a small smile peeked through and she shook her head.

"I'm not sure."

He looked around again. "Did you make all this?"

"No. My father did."

"And who are those for?" he said, gesturing to the bag she held.

"The orphanage director. It's my private donation."

"Well then, let's go deliver it, shall we?"

Her smile widened and she nodded. He held the door open for her, taking one last look before following her out to the hallway.

"What is this?" he asked, waving his arm toward the tunnel.

"Just an extension of the cellars."

"What's behind those doors?"

She led him back to the stairs. "Nothing. They are closed off. That storeroom is the only one we use."

She seemed to be regretting letting him in on her little secret. As well she should. Though what he'd do with the information, he had no idea. If The Red Phoenix was using Jessie's father's old stores, then they weren't buying from Willie. And despite the storeroom of hooch, he hadn't seen any sign of a still.

So. What did he really have? Jameson would be thrilled with a storeroom of booze, but technically it wasn't illegal to own. Her father had made it before Prohibition had gone into effect and as long as Jessie wasn't selling it, which he had no real evidence of her doing, then the presence of the room itself was worthless to them.

But she'd shown a great deal of trust in letting him see it. There had been no need for her to show him. But she had. Why?

To see his reaction perhaps? Test him? See if he'd go running off to Jameson?

He took a deep breath. It was an important discovery, but until he knew what to do with it, he would just act like it was none of his beeswax. He didn't want Jameson harassing her more than he already was. Tony hadn't seen one thing to indicate that Jessie even knew a man named the Phoenix, let alone was his partner or lover. All he'd seen was a hardworking, charitable woman who could sing like an angel and kiss like the devil.

He'd keep what he'd discovered to himself until she gave him a reason for sharing it.

"Oh, I didn't put out the lamp," she said, turning to go back down.

"I'll get it," Tony said. "It'll just take a second."

Jessie hesitated, but Tony had already turned and was

heading back down to the storeroom. He listened, but didn't hear her following him. He pulled the Vest Pocket Kodak camera Jameson had given him out of his suit pocket, flipping it open and cursing when the bellows stuck a bit. He fiddled with it, finally getting them to extend fully and quickly snapped some pictures of the storeroom, hating himself a little more with every click.

The pictures wouldn't harm her. They were no proof that she was selling anything. Hell, the Feds probably wouldn't be able to see anything in the tiny pictures anyway. But they were *something* and might get Jameson off his back, buy him a little more time. He had to give the man something or they'd yank him off the job and then he wouldn't be able to help Jessie, or find out what was really going on.

"Tony?" Jessie called down.

Tony put out the lamp, shoving the camera back in his pocket. Maybe he wouldn't need to give Jameson the pictures at all. He could find another way to stay on the job *and* get to the bottom of things. No one ever need see them.

"Sorry," he said when he got back to the top. "It was dark down there without the light."

The smile Jessie bestowed on him both warmed his heart and made him cringe. He never should have taken those pictures. It was a horrible impulse that he should never have acted on.

She grabbed his tie and pulled him down for a long, lingering kiss.

"Thank you, Tony."

He kissed the tip of her nose. "We'd best get moving."

He took the satchel from her and led her from the store to his waiting car, guilt lapping at his heels.

Chapter Fourteen

Jessie took her place, keeping her eyes down even after the heat of the spotlight hit her. Even after several weeks of singing, she still couldn't calm the stampede of elephants in her belly. Until the first notes of her song rang out. Each note seemed to chase away a little more of her fear and by the time the introduction blended into the opening notes of the song, she was fully ready to let loose.

She opened her mouth and sang, filling her diaphragm and letting her voice carry through every corner of the speakeasy. Her body swayed in time to the music and Jessie let the tempo dictate her movements. It was a fun song, a bit cheeky. The singer sang it with a playful, kittenish voice. But not Jessie.

Jessie had the band slow the music down. Her voice was deeper, richer, and made the lyrics somehow less flirty and infinitely more naughty. She swayed her shoulders and shook her hips as the song dictated, but with the slower rhythm, her movements were borderline indecent. And she reveled in it. She never stepped out of line in her real life. So for the few moments she was on stage, it was wickedly fun to vamp it up.

Her eyes roved over the crowd as she sang. Until they came to rest on Tony.

He stood at the back of the room, leaning against the bar with a tumbler of rum in his hand, his eyes locked onto hers. All the other patrons disappeared. It was only her and him in the room, her voice meant only for him. When she sang the line about letting someone take a kiss, Tony's teeth scraped along his lower lip. The sight of him biting his lip sent a wave of heat through her that almost turned her knees to jelly, and she no longer needed to put on an act to sell the song to her audience. Every word of it was the truth. The riot of sensation rocking through her body lent a rasping sultriness to her voice that had her audience mesmerized. But she had eyes for only Tony.

He put his glass down on the bar, walked slowly around the outskirts of the tables, across the dance floor where a few couples were moving together in time to the song. Jessie kept him in her sights, her eyes following him as he moved closer to her.

Jessie's voice lingered on the last notes, making sure Tony's eyes were riveted on hers. Her hands glided down her body until they hung straight at her side. For one more moment, the magic of the song encapsulated her and Tony. And then the applause rang out from the audience, shattering the illusion.

Jessie stared out at her new, adoring fans and tried not to panic. She'd acted like a complete tart! Though they seemed to love her for it, she was embarrassed at how carried away she'd let herself get.

One of the men from the audience jumped up, whistling and hooting so loudly his drunken companions were practically rolling on the floor with their laughter.

"Sing another one, baby!"

Maybe it was time for a break. Jessie eyed the man warily, her stomach doing a queasy flip. She took another little bow and stepped away from the microphone. The man took several lurching steps toward the stage. Jessie looked around, trying to find Tony, but with the spotlight in her face she couldn't see anything but the hulking drunkard coming toward her.

"Where you goin'?" he slurred. "Sing another one for me!"

He stumbled up onto the stage, his big meaty paw swiping at her. Jessie jumped back, a startled squeak all she could muster past the panic that squeezed at her throat. He got ahold of her wrist and dragged her up against him. A mingled chorus of boos and catcalls rose from the audience.

"Hey now!" Louis said, coming to her rescue. The man brushed him off, shoving him back, and the other band members marched forward.

"You can be bad with me anytime, baby," he said, his rum-laden breath making her stomach turn as it wafted over her. "Why don't we go somewhere a little more priv—"

Before he could finish his sentence, Tony's hand clamped to the back of his collar and he hauled him off her. He swung the drunkard around, right into the waiting arms of the club's burly bouncer. It only took a matter of seconds, but Jessie was shaking like a newborn kitten.

Tony wrapped an arm around her waist. He turned a smiling face to the audience, though Jessie noticed that it didn't match his eyes. His entire body was rigid with rage.

"Jessie Harlan, ladies and gentleman!"

The applause rang out again and Tony stood back a little, though he didn't let her go, and let the audience praise her.

Then he stepped back to the microphone. "Miss Harlan will be back in a few short minutes to continue the show. I'll leave you in the capable hands of our band."

Before Jessie could protest, Louis started a new song and

Tony whisked her off to his office.

The second the door was closed he ran his hands over her, checking her for injuries. He brushed her hair back to look into her eyes. Then, with a frustrated groan, Tony dragged her to him and kissed her, his lips tenderly moving over hers until she trembled in his arms.

When he released her, she wasn't sure if her limbs shook from the incident on the stage or from Tony's soft, warm lips.

"Are you all right? You aren't hurt, are you?" he asked, taking her hand and looking at her wrist.

Jessie blew out a tremulous breath, the fear thundering through her bloodstream slowly dissipating. "Yes, I'm fine. Thanks to you."

"What did you think you were doing?"

"Excuse me?" She still floated in an overly sensitized haze, could still taste him on her lips, and his abrupt change of subject left her reeling. "I didn't…I mean you were the one who…"

Tony paced to his desk, then back to her. Jessie frowned at him, thoroughly confused by his sudden change of mood.

"That song. The way you sang it."

"You don't like that song?"

"No, it's not that… That song you sang. I'm not sure that was the best choice."

"Haven't we had this conversation before?"

Tony almost smiled and Jessie bit her lip to keep from smiling.

"Well, it appears you haven't learned your lesson yet." He pulled her against him and she sucked in a breath.

"That song is all the rage right now. I thought the crowd would like it."

"They obviously did. Some more than others. That man could have hurt you if I hadn't gotten there in time."

Jessie waved him off. "Louis was right there, and so was

your bouncer. I would have been fine."

"Jessie…"

She couldn't keep from smiling. "You seemed to enjoy it well enough."

He stared at her, his irritation melting into something much more sensual. His smile grew and he pressed closer, showing her exactly how well he enjoyed it. "Is this what you had in mind, Miss Harlan, when you sang that song to me?"

He nipped at her lip and Jessie's breath caught in her throat.

"Yes. I mean, no," she said when he chuckled, the low, rumbling laugh full of virile male pride and heat. "I…I wasn't singing to you, I just…"

He brushed his lips along hers, then deepened the kiss until all Jessie could feel and think about was his mouth against hers, the taste of the rum on his tongue, the silky softness of his hair sliding through her fingers.

"Is this what you want, Jessie?"

His voice had grown husky and sent shivers down her spine. Or maybe it was his lips trailing down her neck that was doing that? Or the way he nibbled at the pulse jumping in her throat?

Oh yes, this was exactly what she wanted.

His lips covered hers before she had half a second to think and he kissed her with a vigor that shocked her. She'd wanted to torment him, but she'd never dreamed she'd be quite so successful. Her surprise melted into desire as his onslaught continued and she kissed him back, pouring into it every ounce of passion, desire, fear, and anxiety that had been tumbling around inside her for the past few weeks.

His hand came up to cup her face, his thumb stroking down along her jaw, gently pressing on her chin until she opened to him. He explored her mouth until only his hard body pressed against hers kept her from slumping to the floor on legs that no longer wanted to hold her.

He leaned his forehead against hers and she was happy to find that she wasn't the only one breathing as though she'd just run up a flight of stairs. He pulled away, his eyes burning into hers, and waited. She knew what he was doing. Giving her the chance to stop, to walk away. And she knew she should. But it would have been easier to cut off her own leg than walk away from him.

Instead, Jessie ran her hands up Tony's chest, over the lapels of his suit, up the rock hard column of his neck where his pulse beat against her hand as though it would burst from his skin. She smiled, loving that his heart pounded for *her*. Then she slipped her fingers into his hair and pulled him back to her, drawing his tongue inside her mouth, tasting every inch of him, until their slow and steady kiss was no longer enough for either of them.

Tony's hand dragged up her thigh, hiking her dress up with it, and the first brush of his hand on her bare skin had Jessie gasping his name. She brought her leg up to wrap around his waist and he bent, lifting her into his arms so she could wrap the other around him as well.

He pressed her back against the wall, letting the full hardness of his body rock against her aching core, and she arched into him with a moan. He covered her mouth with his own, swallowing down her cries as he kissed her. She yanked at his bow tie, tore at the buttons on his shirt, wanting, *needing*, to feel his skin against hers.

Jessie didn't know where this frantic desire came from that had to be met before she went insane. She knew she should stop. She *knew* it would bring her nothing but trouble. But every brush of Tony's lips against her skin made her care less and less.

She had never felt like this with Mario. Had never felt this instant rush of fire that ignited every inch of her body.

There had been excitement, and enough heat to lead her to do things she wasn't ready for. But nothing like this inferno that threatened to consume her. She whimpered, clutching at Tony, not even sure what she wanted, only knowing he was the only one who could give it to her.

The pounding of someone's fist on the door startled them both into awareness of their surroundings. Tony let her slide down the length of his body, setting her dress to rights while they both struggled to catch their breath.

Someone knocked again. "Boss? You in there?"

"Yeah, whaddya want?" Tony growled.

"The crowd's getting a little restless. Will Miss Harlan be going back on tonight?"

Tony glanced at her and Jessie gave him a small nod. "She'll be out in a few."

"All right, boss. I'll tell the band."

Jessie leaned her head against Tony's chest, both relieved and disappointed that they'd been interrupted. She'd been ready to let him take her right there against the wall in his office. She couldn't imagine what he must think of her. And yet, with every nerve ending still on fire and begging for his touch, she didn't regret her actions. Only that they'd been interrupted.

Tony straightened her dress, brushed her hair back from her face, and then pulled her gently into his arms, pressing a kiss to her forehead before his lips moved lower, kissing each cheek, trailing to her neck, to the hollow behind her ear. The tension built again, an aching burn that begged to be inflamed.

But reality had intruded and as much as she hated it, she knew she had to be smart and keep her head about her. She wanted Tony. More than she'd ever wanted any other man in her life. But now wasn't the time. Not when all their secrets hung over their heads. It took more effort than she cared to admit, but she gently pushed him away.

"This isn't a good idea, Tony."

Tony wrapped his hands around her waist and pulled her back against him, leaning down so he could whisper in her ear. "We might have to agree to disagree on that point, Jessie. But I'll give you a fair warning. Unless you want to spend a lot more of your time in this office with me…" He ran a hand up her back, tangling his fingers in her hair. "Then you might want to be more careful with your song choices."

Oh, yes. They'd definitely had this conversation before. Only she hadn't really taken his warning to heart. And she wasn't sure she wanted to this time. Still, she answered, "I'll keep that in mind."

"You do that." Tony leaned down, tugging on her hair enough that she had to tilt her head up to keep it from pulling. His mouth descended and he kissed her again until she was almost sobbing for more.

Someone pounded on the door again. "Hey boss. Got a situation out here."

Tony growled and let her go. He yanked the door open, leaving her trembling against the wall.

She brought her hand up to her mouth and smiled. She would certainly keep that in mind.

Chapter Fifteen

The late nights were going to kill her. All she really wanted to do was curl up in the corner and sleep for a week. Charlie was helping out a lot, but he wasn't able to fill in full time. Jessie might need to hire someone else if she was going to continue to sing at The Corkscrew and run things at The Red Phoenix. Luckily, Joe had things under control at The Red Phoenix the nights she wasn't there, but she was still taking care of all of the paperwork and administrative tasks, as well as working at the club the nights she wasn't at The Corkscrew. She was wearing pretty thin. Perhaps she'd put an ad in the paper today for more help at the shop.

She slumped on the counter, banging her head against it a couple times. Why did she continue this? If she had any brains at all, she'd pack it up and get out of town. But a quick look around the shop where she'd grown up answered that question for her. This was her home. This shop was all she had left of her father. She couldn't just leave it.

But she could close the speakeasy. Soon. She almost had the money she needed to finish paying off Willie *with* enough tucked away to ensure that she'd never have to worry about losing her father's shop—no matter how slow business got. Once she had that security in place, she'd close The Red Phoenix and go back to being a full time butcher. Maybe she'd add a deli. And some baked goods.

Jessie smiled, enjoying her dreams of a simpler life. Someday, hopefully soon, she'd have that life. For now, it was time to close up shop and get ready to perform.

She couldn't stop the quiver of pleasure that hit her at the thought of seeing Tony again. She sighed. The man was handsome enough to stop traffic. But he didn't belong in her world. More to the point, she didn't belong in his. In the Phoenix's world, maybe they could coexist. Though, there he was her rival. Only interested in her for the information he could glean on the Phoenix. And that world wasn't real. In this world, in her *real* world, she wasn't sure if they belonged together. But, maybe they could overcome their differences, their pasts, and build something new together.

When the bell tinkled over her shop door, Jessie wearily dragged herself off the counter to help whoever had come in. She looked up to greet her customer and immediately froze. She was sure the smile she'd plastered on her face was more of a grimace and she tried hard to relax it into something more natural. Not so easy when one of the goons for the most ruthless bootlegger in the city was smiling at you from the other side of the counter. The fact he was her ex didn't help either.

"Mario. What do you want?"

He removed his gloves and leaned against the counter, slapping them against his hand.

"That's not a very polite way to greet an old friend."

"I'm not sure what else you expect."

"A kiss might be nice." He leaned against the counter and gave her a look that had once turned her knees to jelly.

Mario had the dark and handsome thing going on, though he wasn't as tall as Tony. And where Tony's ruggedly handsome features filled Jessie with heat, like he was her own personal smoldering fire, Mario's good looks were cold and distant, like a statue of some Greek god. Attractive, striking even, but there was no warmth beneath the surface. Something she wished she'd realized sooner.

"That's not going to happen, Mario."

"Well, a man can hope, eh?"

Jessie could remember the feel of his sinfully full lips pressing against hers, his hands hot and urgent on her skin. The memory filled her with revulsion now. She'd thought she was in love with him. Would have done anything for him. A fact he had exploited to the fullest. Jessie had told him everything, given up everything to him, all her secrets, all of *her*.

And he'd used her like a worthless piece of trash. Something Jessie hadn't been aware of until after they'd been dating for several months and she'd caught him in bed with some nameless floozy.

Though what had really done her in was when he'd brought her to Willie's attention. Escorted the man right through the front door of The Red Phoenix and parked him at the best table in the house. Being in debt to Willie had been bad enough. But at least all she'd had to do was drop discreet payments once a month in a mailbox uptown.

Being on his radar as a rival was intolerable. Mario hadn't just broken her heart; he'd tried his best to ruin her life. The man was scum. And she couldn't let her full feelings show because he was still Willie's man and his goodwill could go a long way to making her life livable. Literally.

Thankfully, some small spark of self-preservation had kicked in and kept her from spilling all the beans about her club. Mario had known about The Red Phoenix and her involvement. But she hadn't told him *she* was the Phoenix.

Thank God.

So now, like everyone else, Willie thought she was just the current skirt the Phoenix was playing with. One he trusted enough to oversee things, but still, someone with very little power. And Jessie wanted to keep it that way. If they knew *she* was the Phoenix…she shuddered, trying to keep that thought at bay.

Jessie crossed her arms and waited.

"You're late with your payment. I was sent to see if you needed any…assistance."

"Oh! I'm sorry, I've been so busy, I forgot. I have it…"

"I should hope so, for your sake." All trace of the charming guy she'd fallen for was gone, replaced by the coldhearted enforcer he really was.

Jessie swallowed. Her heart nearly in her throat. "It's in my office. If you could just wait for a moment?"

Mario's eyes narrowed, but he nodded. Jessie hurried down the stairs into the cellar and yanked open the door to the refrigerated room. The envelope with Willie's payoff money was stashed between two slats near the door. She took a second to lean against the cool wall, trying to catch her breath.

How could she have been so stupid? It was bad enough to forget to pay a regular creditor, but to forget to pay Willie…it was tantamount to suicide.

Luckily, she'd been pulling in enough that she had a triple payment for him. That might ease some of his irritation at having to send one of his guys out to collect. Hopefully it wouldn't pique his interest in her club. The tightrope she had to walk to keep all the jackals at bay was giving her stomach pains. The payment should be just enough to make Willie happy without being so much that he worried her speakeasy was becoming too much of a rival for his own.

She hoped she could make a similar payment the next

month, which would pay Willie off once and for all. She would be glad to be free of at least one of the blades that seemed to be hanging over her head. And hopefully she'd never have to set eyes on Mario again.

She ran back up the stairs and slid the envelope across the counter. "Please convey my apologies. There is a triple payment in there. And I hope to be able to make the same next month, which should clear my debt."

Mario cracked open the envelope and did a quick count, thumbing through the bills stacked inside.

"Very good. I was instructed to educate you on the importance of being punctual…"

Rigid with fear, Jessie stood her ground. She wouldn't show Mario how terrified she was. It was like with bees and dogs… Willie's goons could smell fear and it only spurred them on.

"However, since it does seem to just be an oversight, and since I'm still rather fond of you and all of your…softer parts," he said, a little of his come-hither charm oozing back into his voice as his gaze raked over her, "*and* since you have an overpayment, no less, I think we can let this slide. I advise you not to let it happen again. Not even my influence will keep Willie at bay should he decide you need a lesson in good manners. And that face of yours is just too pretty to mess up, *hmm*?"

Jessie nodded, adrenaline making her knees weak. She put a trembling hand on the counter to steady herself. "It won't happen again."

"Good," Mario said, slipping the envelope into his pocket. "Word is you're singing at The Corkscrew now."

Jessie's eyebrow cocked. "Word travels fast."

He gave her an appraising look. "We were surprised to hear of it."

"We?"

Mario pinned her with a look and Jessie dropped the act. They both knew she knew exactly to whom he referred. She gave him a faint smile, trying to keep her stomach from revolting in sheer terror. She'd been getting more and more on Willie's bad side with every successful night at her club. Willie didn't mind a little competition, as long as that competition stayed *little*. And bought Willie's booze to fuel that success. But The Red Phoenix didn't buy from Willie and entirely too many people were frequenting the club for Willie's taste.

Russo was waiting for her to respond, so she shrugged. "I'm not sure why Willie is interested in where I choose to sing."

"Willie is interested in the Phoenix. And if his best gal is abandoning him for a rival…well, that interests Willie greatly."

Jessie's gaze darted around. "I haven't abandoned the Phoenix."

"Then that is even more troubling to hear. The Phoenix is a nuisance right now, but if he were to team up with another owner, combine resources…"

"No, no. That's not it at all. I'm just singing a few nights at a different club, that's all. I always wanted to sing, but The Red Phoenix already has a singer, so…" Jessie heard herself rambling and zipped her lip.

Mario studied her for a moment, his sharp eyes taking in everything. "So, the Phoenix sent you in to spy on the competition, eh?"

Jessie kept her composure. She always tried to give Willie just enough information to make it seem as though she was cooperating without giving away too much. It was a fine, but incredibly dangerous, not to mention hair-raising, line to walk.

Mario nodded his head. "Smart man." He straightened, pulled his gloves back on and fixed her with a stare. "Keeping an eye on one's competition is always a good move if you want to stay in business."

She straightened her back, held her head high and gave him a sharp nod. She knew exactly what he was saying. Willie would be keeping his eye on her.

"He must have a lot of faith in you, Jessie."

Jessie knew she should just keep her mouth shut and let the man leave, but she couldn't stop from asking, "Why?"

Mario shook his head. "If you were still my broad and were spending all your time with some P.I., I'd be a little worried you were going to do me wrong. But then you," he said, leaning across the counter and running a finger down her cheek, "would never bite the hand that feeds you, would you?"

"What are you talking about?"

"You mean you don't know?" he asked, with a tone that suggested he was all too aware of her ignorance.

Jessie's stomach sank. She wasn't sure she wanted to hear what he had to say.

"Your new boss, the one you've been getting so cozy with. He's an ex-cop. Got fired when a case went bad. He's since gone into private investigating. Until just recently, when he threw his hat in the speakeasy game. Know any reason why he might have a sudden interest in the illegal side of life?"

Jessie's head spun, as if all the blood had drained from her body, leaving her hot and cold at the same time. Her face was stone. She couldn't have forced an expression on it if she'd tried.

Mario gave her a small smile and pulled an envelope out of his jacket pocket. "You might want to tell any parties who may be interested that keeping the wrong sort of company can be dangerous to one's health."

Jessie took the envelope and nodded.

Russo's smile widened, though the expression never made it past the dead calm of his eyes. "We'll be watching the company you keep, baby. You might want to be a little more discerning in whom you choose to spend your time with. The wrong friends could bring a world of trouble down on you." He leaned forward, his hand cupping the back of her head, and pressed a kiss to her unresponsive lips. Her reaction, or lack thereof, didn't bother him in the slightest. He gave her a final grin, tipped his hat to her, and left.

Jessie opened the envelope and what was left of the blood in her head evacuated. She sank onto a stool and stared at the newspaper clipping in her hand. A picture of Tony, his face turned from the camera, his hand held up to block the lens. But she could still make out his face.

The article described the case Mario had mentioned. A sting operation gone bad. Tony's partner had been shot and killed and after the investigation, Tony had retired from the force. The only other thing in the envelope was a business card. For Anthony Solomon, Private Investigator.

Jessie wasn't sure what to think, what to do. She'd been aware that Tony might have been in cahoots with Jameson, but his actions over the last few weeks had seemed to disprove that assumption. After she'd allowed him to find part of her cache, she'd waited for Jameson to come storming into the shop and lead her away in cuffs. But the more days that passed without that happening, the more Jessie had begun to believe that Tony was exactly what he said. A speakeasy owner who was possibly starting to fall for her.

She had been such a fool.

• • •

Tony snapped another picture and then watched Russo walk out of Jessie's shop with a growing spark of anger gnawing at his gut. He didn't know what that palooka had been doing in there, but it couldn't be anything good. Jessie had looked disturbingly comfortable with the man, considering their past. When he'd stroked her face and kissed her, Tony had wanted to bust through the door and rip Russo's hand off. But that would have betrayed the fact that he'd been watching them. Besides, she hadn't seemed to mind. A fact that made Tony want to put his fist through a wall. He knew he was overreacting. He had no claim on her. In fact, if she knew who he really was and what he was doing, she'd hate him.

He took a deep breath and rubbed his hands over his face. He hadn't meant to spy on her. Hadn't meant to take pictures of her meeting with anyone. But, he'd pulled up just as Russo was going into the shop. Why would Russo be meeting with her again? Everything Tony had heard had led him to believe their relationship was over. If she was the Phoenix's girl now, Russo was throwing down an awfully big gauntlet walking into his dame's shop.

Then again, Russo was also Willie's guy and Willie was interested in Jessie for all the same reasons Tony was. Maybe he was just using Russo as a means to an end. Either way, Tony wasn't about to just drive away, so he'd parked down the block and watched from a distance, in case she needed him. Which she hadn't.

Tony looked back toward the shop and saw Jessie shoving the envelope the mook had given her into her apron pocket. What could that be? Bribe money? A payoff of some sort? Willie wouldn't be buying her booze. But she must have something of interest to him because he'd seemed pleased with the envelope she'd pushed across the counter to him. Was it information? Maybe the same information Tony himself was trying to get ahold of?

The moment that thought crossed his mind, he realized that Jameson had never mentioned trying to buy information about the Phoenix from Jessie. He'd interrogated her, threatened her, sent Tony in to romance her. But he'd never, that Tony was aware of, tried to buy her off. The thought had never occurred to Tony either, which now seemed unusual. Everyone had their price. Jessie must have hers, too. And apparently Willie had found out what it was.

Tony stowed his camera in his car and marched over to the shop. Jessie had flipped the CLOSED sign but she hadn't locked the door yet, so Tony let himself in, locking the door behind him so they wouldn't be disturbed.

Jessie turned when the door opened, but her eyes didn't light up to see him as they had before. Her gaze darted around but she at least made a pretense of smiling at him.

"You're closing up late," he said.

"I had a straggler come in."

"Ah. A regular? Come in for a little chat just when you were ready to close." Tony tried to force a smile, keep his tone lighthearted.

"No, he wasn't someone I know. He was just…asking directions to the nearest deli. He was looking for some dinner and didn't realize I didn't sell anything pre-made."

His stomach sank even while his anger sparked anew. If the meeting had been innocent, if Russo was still her enemy, surely she would have told him, confided in him. Asked him for help, maybe. Instead, she'd denied even knowing the man, when it had been obvious, even from the outside, that that wasn't the case.

"Well, that's too bad that you didn't get anything from him," Tony said.

Jessie twitched, her hand straying toward her pocket. "What do you mean?"

"A sale. He came in and talked your ear off without even buying anything. Not very polite."

"Oh," Jessie said, the relief in her slight laugh the only genuine expression she'd made since he'd walked in. "No, not very polite. Tony," she said, her brow crinkling. "What did you do before you started running The Corkscrew?"

Tony froze. Why was she asking this now? Is that what Willie had paid her for? Information on him?

"I was a bartender before Prohibition, believe it or not. And I've done a few odd jobs here and there since then."

"So running a speakeasy must have come naturally to you."

"A bit," he said with a faint smile.

"How did you end up running The Corkscrew?"

Tony admired her style. No beating around the bush like he'd been doing. Just straight and direct. Maybe he should have tried that approach with her. Though she seemed to be growing paler and more agitated with every question she asked. The knot in his stomach eased up a bit. Whatever was going on with her, whoever was paying her off, Tony didn't think it sat well with her. She wasn't acting like a person who was an expert in this game.

"The old owner was an acquaintance of mine."

"I see," she said, her voice faint.

Tony frowned. Whatever game she was playing was taking a toll on her. He reached over and caressed her face, purposely following the same path the other man had taken, as if he could erase the man's touch from her skin.

"What's wrong, Jessie?"

She blinked up at him, her eyes suspiciously bright. For just a moment she leaned into his hand.

"Tell me what's going on. Maybe I can help you," he said.

Jessie let out a long, quiet sigh. "No. You can't help me."

Tony was about to protest, insist that she tell him what was going on. But Jessie forced a smile. "It's nothing, I promise. I'm just tired, that's all."

Tony studied her for a second but she made no move to say anything else.

"All right, then. I'll see you at the club."

Jessie nodded and walked him to the door.

"Goodnight, Jessie."

He wished he could scoop her up in his arms, take her upstairs, and just forget about the mess they'd gotten themselves into. He hesitated, then leaned in, unable to help himself.

Jessie turned her head and his lips brushed against her cheek. Tony pulled back, his heart clenching like she'd reached into his chest and wrenched it out. He stepped back, jaw rigid, doing his best to keep her from seeing his hurt. His eyes narrowed as he searched her features, trying to find some clue to what was going on in her head. She refused to meet his gaze and a rising anger compounded the ache that tightened his chest. *What the hell was going on?*

"Goodnight, Tony."

Her voice sounded so small, so sad. Tony shoved aside his feelings and reached for her, rubbing his thumb across her cheek and pulling her closer to press a kiss to her forehead. She relaxed into him for a split second before stiffening in his arms. He released her. Then he walked out her door, hoping that it wasn't for the last time.

Chapter Sixteen

Jameson looked up in surprise when Tony entered his office the next day.

"Well, now. Finally stopping in to give me an update, *hmm*? About damn time."

Tony grimaced but wasn't about to argue with the man. "I think you need to put a larger detail on Jessie…or pull her in, offer her a deal."

"Has something happened?"

"Willie's getting a little too close for comfort."

Jameson's eyes widened. "Have you seen the Harlan girl with one of Willie's guys?"

Tony pressed his lips together, not wanting to give Jameson any ammo to work with, especially since he wasn't sure there was any yet.

"You going to tell me what this is about?"

"Not sure there is anything to tell yet."

"Well, it's gotta be something or you wouldn't be in here."

Tony took a deep breath. "Russo has been sniffing around."

Jameson gave a low whistle. "Mario Russo? Where did you run into him? The shop?"

"No."

Jameson glowered at Tony. "Sit. Now."

Tony slowly sat down, gritting his teeth hard enough to chip a tooth. He didn't know the best course of action to take and being at a loss was not something he was used to. The more he'd gotten to know Jessie, the less he'd considered her a threat. Hell, the woman practically fainted before every performance. There was no way she was a hardened criminal. And he'd been almost convinced enough to tell Jameson so.

Until he saw her getting up close and personal with one of Willie's main guys.

Now, what he thought he knew had gone all to hell and the last person he wanted in his face saying, "I told you so," was Jameson.

Jameson sat behind his desk and leaned forward, linking his hands together. "Where did you see Mario Russo?"

Tony sucked in a breath through his nose. Unless he flat-out lied to Jameson, he wasn't going to be able to get away with keeping Jessie out of this. And he wasn't even sure he should.

"Solomon, we have worked too hard and spent too much damn money on this case to come up empty now. I swear to God if you don't start squawkin' and spill everything you've found out about that woman and who she works for, I'll personally make sure you never investigate anything more important than a lost poodle again. Your career will be over. You understand me?"

Tony glared, his jaw aching from clenching it so tight. But he jerked his head in a semblance of a nod.

"Now, let's try this again. Where did you see Mario Russo?"

What he was about to say made him physically ill. But he

didn't have a choice. And the way things were looking, Jessie probably deserved to be turned over. He'd known from the start she was hiding something. He just never imagined how far her subterfuge might go.

"I saw him meeting with Jessie in her shop last night."

The delight that lit up Jameson's face sent a rush of fury through Tony so hot that he had to grip the arms of his chair to keep from wrapping his hands around Jameson's throat.

"Finally!" Jameson slammed his hands down on the table. "We've got her."

"We don't have anything. We've got a guy walking into a butcher shop and then walking back out ten minutes later. Hardly damning evidence. We have no idea what they were discussing."

"Then you need to find out. You and I both know that a man like Russo isn't going to be out running his own errands. If he was there visiting your little skirt, then it was pure business and I guarantee it wasn't legal."

"He might have been threatening her."

"So what if he was?"

Tony's face must have betrayed his rising fury because Jameson actually sat back in his chair.

"For all we know they never split up. Or maybe he wants her back. What difference does it make? Unless you have any hard evidence that her life is in danger, we aren't going to make a move and risk blowing everything we've set up here. I don't know what the hell you've got going on with that dame," he said, "but you were paid to find out the dirt. If your methods have bitten you in the ass, that's your own fault and you can just deal with it. But mark my words, if you keep any pertinent information from me that will impede this investigation, I'll not only have your career, I'll throw your damn ass behind bars."

"I'm not hiding anything."

"Good. Because I stuck my neck out for you to get you this gig. The last thing either of us needs is for this to turn into another Lucille situation. Got it?"

The mention of Lucille was like a bucket of ice water being dumped on Tony's head. He *was* defending Jessie the same way he'd done with Lucille. And look where that had gotten him. At least with Lucille he hadn't had any hard evidence. He couldn't say the same about Jessie. What he had might be speculative and circumstantial, but it was certainly enough to prove something was going on. Yet here he was, caught in the same trap.

He rubbed his hand over his face, wishing he'd never agreed to this damn job. What the hell was the right thing to do? He didn't want to lean too far in the other direction and ruin Jessie's life if there was really nothing going on.

No, maybe he didn't need to hand over everything he had on Jessie just yet. But he could give Jameson something. Until he found out the truth about Jessie.

"As I was saying," Jameson continued, "if she was being threatened by him that just proves that she's dirty. Willie's men don't go around threatening innocent women. If Russo is in there leaning on her, then there is a reason for it, don't you think?"

Tony nodded. He hated to admit it, but Jameson had a point.

"She didn't look like she was being threatened," he said. "In fact, they looked…friendly."

Jameson leaned forward again. "Well, now. That *is* interesting. If he were threatening her, it would be reasonable to assume that she and the Phoenix, if there *is* a Phoenix, were encroaching on his territory. But a friendly visit…well that implies a nice, working relationship, doesn't it? Or a relationship of some sort, anyway. Did you speak with her after you saw this?"

"Yes. She seemed shaken."

Jameson waved that off. "That could be chalked up to you walking in minutes after Russo left. She must have been wondering if you'd seen him."

Tony had thought the same thing, but he didn't feel the need to let Jameson know that. He was cooperating, but he didn't have to go overboard with it.

"What do you mean, if there is a Phoenix?"

Jameson looked at him like he was a complete dumkuff. "There have been rumors about the Phoenix for as long as the speakeasy has been open. But no one has ever seen the man. No one. Except Miss Harlan. Have you seen or heard any evidence at all to suggest that he exists?"

The answer was no. Jessie spent all day at her shop and nights in either his club or The Red Phoenix. That didn't mean that the Phoenix wasn't running things at The Red Phoenix while Jessie was with him, but what kind of man let his woman out of his sight for that long? Let her work at a rival speakeasy? And why hadn't he ever been seen, even in his own club? Tony had heard of keeping a low profile, but this was crazy.

But the alternative was something that Tony had tried hard not to consider. Because if there was no Phoenix, that meant that Jessie was the one in charge. And that complicated his life to a degree he didn't think he could recover from.

"That's what I thought," Jameson said, not needing to hear from Tony what they both already knew. "Anything else happen?"

Tony sighed. "They exchanged envelopes. Russo came in and Jessie hurried off and came back with one which she gave to him. They spoke for awhile and then Russo handed her an envelope."

Jameson grimaced. "Well now, that's fairly important information, Solomon. Might have been best to lead off with that. That settles it then. She's on Willie's payroll."

"That doesn't settle anything. We don't even know what was in the envelope. For all we know, they were exchanging recipes."

"Unlikely."

"Maybe. But we've got no evidence of anything just yet. I'm the only witness that Russo was even there. It'd be his word against mine. And we've got no proof that he gave her anything."

Tony didn't mention that he had pictures of the whole transaction.

"Then you'll just have to go get some proof, won't you? We are too close to this to lose it now, Solomon. Whatever personal feelings you have about this, forget them. You've got a job to do."

Tony stood and headed for the door.

"And Solomon."

He stopped, only turning half around.

"I'll expect you to come back with something soon. This has been dragging on long enough. Finish it."

Tony left before he planted his fist in Jameson's face.

• • •

Jessie sat at her desk, reading over the newspaper clipping for what was probably the hundredth time. She didn't know what to do about it. On the one hand, she hated to judge anyone for his past. Everyone made mistakes. Some larger than others. But still, if she condemned everyone who had screwed up in the past, she'd never be able to trust anyone, including herself. On the other hand, Tony used to be a cop. With close ties to the Feds. It meant he knew Jameson, not because Jameson was harassing him but because they used to be on the same team. And very likely still were.

The most probable scenario was what she'd thought all along, one that she had shied away from because thinking it caused an ache in her chest that made it difficult to breathe. That Tony had been trying to get close to her in order to get information out of her. Only he didn't want it for himself, but for his buddy Jameson. And the romance? All those lingering glances and kisses that made the seams on her stockings curl? What were they? Was it real? Did he care for her? Or desire her, at least? Or was it all part of his ploy?

She should be angry, furious. But instead she was filled with an infinite sadness that rolled over her in bitter waves, lapping at the happiness she'd thought for a moment she might find.

This is why she'd never let anyone get too close. If you let people in, they used you, then threw you away. She was better off alone. At least, if she was alone she wouldn't feel this crushing sorrow that leeched into her heart and destroyed her from the inside out.

She shoved the clipping in a drawer and closed up her office, heading back into the tunnels beneath the shop's cellar. Maybe it was time to end her singing career. Cut ties with Tony before they got any closer. Especially with Willie sniffing around and making not-so-veiled threats. She should end it all. Before Tony had a chance to hurt her worse than she was already hurting. The thought of not seeing him anymore made her heart ache. But better an ache now than shattered pieces later.

"Jessie?" Joe called to her from the storeroom.

She followed the sound of his voice and found him packing a few cases for the night ahead at The Red Phoenix.

"Not too much longer," she said, running her hand down one of the empty shelves. There wasn't much left in here. She had more than enough to keep the club running for several more years, squirreled away in other rooms. But her plan had always been to shut things down once this room was empty. Just long enough to pay off Willie and ensure her shop could stay on its feet. Judging by the looks of things, she had only enough booze in this room to keep the speakeasy running for another month or two. One more payment to Willie. And then she could close things down. It would be a relief.

Her only worry was Maude. Joe and Charlie would still have their jobs at the shop. But perhaps Maude could take her place at The Corkscrew. They'd need a new singer.

Joe smiled and closed up the last box. "It'll be nice to go back to being butchers."

Jessie laughed. "I was just thinking the same thing."

"We could just give it all away now and be done with it."

"Sure. I think I'll team up with Willie. Give him all the booze."

Joe snorted and Jessie winked at him. They'd already decided long ago not to use the liquor to pay off Willie. All she needed was for the Feds to find out Willie was selling her father's booze and then she'd be in double the trouble she was in now. Safer to pay him in nice, untraceable cash.

"Have you decided on next week's schedule?" Joe asked.

"Yes. Let's open Monday, Thursday, and Friday."

"All right, boss."

"And let's switch to the Barker Street exit this week. We've been using the Dalton Street exit for a couple weeks now. It's about time to change things up."

"I was just going to suggest it."

Jessie smiled. "I knew I kept you around for a reason."

Joe chuckled and then froze when a shadow crossed the door. Jessie spun around. Tony stood there, his hands in his pockets.

"Sorry, I didn't mean to startle you. I called out, but you must not have heard me."

"No, I didn't." She flashed Joe a look. The question wasn't

whether they'd heard Tony, but whether Tony had heard them. She studied him, trying to see any hint that he'd heard what they'd said.

His smile was a bit strained, but then it had been since the night Russo had dropped in.

"Ah, well, sorry," he said again. "I'll just wait for you upstairs."

Jessie nodded. As soon as Tony had disappeared up the stairs she turned to Joe.

"Do you think he heard?" she whispered.

Joe was staring at the stairs behind her. "I don't know. But maybe we should switch the dates, open Tuesday, Wednesday and Saturday, just in case."

Jessie nodded. Part of her wanted to keep the club open on the days she'd mentioned, just so she could find out if Tony would really betray her or not. And if it was only her life at stake she would. But she couldn't endanger her patrons that way.

"Tuesday, Wednesday, and Saturday then. And let's stay with the Dalton exit one more week. Just in case he heard that as well."

"Sure thing, boss."

Jessie nodded, then went up the stairs after Tony.

He sat perched on a stool near the counter but when she entered he got up and kissed her cheek.

"How are you this evening?"

Jessie watched him, wondering if she had really misread him, wondering if it had all been a lie or if some of it had been real.

"Fine."

"Just fine?" he asked with a small smile.

Jessie smiled back. "A little tired, maybe."

"Well, I don't doubt that. You spend all day in this shop, and all night singing at my joint."

"About that…"

Tony smiled a little and looked down briefly before meeting her eyes again. "You don't want to sing for me anymore?"

She gave him a sad smile. "It's not that I don't want to. I've enjoyed it much more than I expected to. It's just…with the shop and…my other responsibilities… It's getting to be a bit too much."

Tony nodded. "That's understandable. I hate to see you go." He took one of her hands and brought it to his lips, keeping her close even after he'd kissed it. "I'd still like to see you, even if you no longer work for me."

Jessie's heart lurched on a twisted wave of hope and she did her best to stamp it down. Still, if she flat out refused him it might raise more questions. Better to go along with it. For now. "I think I'd like that."

"Good," he said with a smile. "It seems like we spend all our time together at my club. Why don't we mix things up a little?"

"What do you mean?" Jessie asked, wariness winding its icy way through her veins.

"Well, you've been to my club. It seems only fair we go to yours."

"You want to come to The Red Phoenix?" Dread settled in her stomach. It was a good thing she hadn't eaten dinner that night or it would have revolted for sure.

Tony shrugged. "Unless there's some reason why I shouldn't. Is there? The Phoenix, perhaps? Will he be there? Or will word get back to him if you were seen with me?"

"No," Jessie said, then hesitated, unsure of how to get out of this without completely giving herself away. If she said no, he'd assume she was hiding something. But she couldn't bring him to the club. Not while his true identity and purpose were up in the air. That was far too dangerous.

Well, maybe there was a way to test him without endangering anyone. They'd already decided to switch the dates the club would open, in case Tony had heard. So, she'd tell him to come on one of those days. If he had heard, then she wouldn't be passing along any information that he didn't already know. And if he hadn't heard…well it didn't matter because the club wouldn't be open that night, anyway.

She'd deal with what would happen after he found out she'd lied to him later. After she found out if she could trust him or not, once and for all.

"No, that sounds fun. How about next Friday. You can meet me here."

Tony went very still, though his face betrayed nothing. "Friday?"

Jessie nodded.

"All right. I'll see you Friday."

Tony hesitated, then pulled her closer, pressing a kiss to her lips that nearly broke her heart. There was the spark of passion that was always present when he touched her, but this kiss…this kiss was sweet and tender, his lips moving slightly over hers.

It didn't feel like he was saying goodnight. It felt like he was saying good-bye.

Chapter Seventeen

"You sure this is the right night? She said it would be open on Wednesday?" Jameson asked, eyeing the dark alley.

"No, she didn't. That's why I'm certain it will be." Tony shoved his hands in his pockets, wanting to be anywhere else in the world but there.

Tony had gone over and over everything, trying to decide the best move. Not just for him, but for Jessie too. She probably wouldn't agree that bringing the Feds in to raid her club was the best course of action, but in the long run, it really was.

If she was in custody, she'd be protected. And she *would* be in custody. Because Tony had also overheard the street names of both the exits. And had men waiting at both of them. But… at least she'd be safe. Willie couldn't touch her. Neither could the Phoenix. If the man even existed, which Tony seriously doubted. It had been Jessie who'd made the decision on what days to open the club. Jessie who kept the place going. Jessie who the employees turned to. If a man named the Phoenix showed up, Tony would eat his hat. And then he would beat the guy to a pulp.

"She might have been telling you the truth. We haven't seen any sign of anyone."

But she hadn't been, and Tony knew it. She'd lied to him, just like Lucille had. He'd do what he could to protect her, but she'd proven again and again that he couldn't trust her. He had proof, which was more than he ever had with Lucille. The realization ran through him like poison, destroying his heart a little piece at a time. But he couldn't ignore it anymore. Wouldn't put anyone in jeopardy again. Well, at least this time no innocents would get hurt because of his misplaced affection for some woman. He'd do the right thing, no matter how much it hurt either one of them.

Tony sucked in a long, slow breath of the cool night air. Another good thing that might come out of this raid…he could get away from Jameson, for good.

"I overheard them say the club would be open on Monday, Thursday and Friday. And she's probably pretty certain I heard them. So it stands to reason that she switched the dates to Tuesday, Wednesday, and Saturday. And just to be certain, I followed Maude Fairfax, her singer, last night. A cab dropped her off near this alley last night around eleven. What else would a dame be doing all dolled up at that time of night, in this spot? They'll be open tonight. She'll be banking on me going by what I overheard."

Jameson scowled. "You'd better be right, Solomon."

Tony shrugged. "If I'm not, there's no harm done. You'll just raid an empty club, like you've done a dozen times before."

"Stick a cork in it, Solomon."

Tony snorted and turned his attention back to the Dalton Street exit. He wasn't sure whether to hope that he was right or wrong. Or whether to hope Jessie made it out or got pinched. Too many what-ifs, no matter which way he looked at it. But none of them had him coming out looking like the good guy. At least, not to Jessie. He'd lose her. But maybe he could save her from herself, and a few bootlegging goons, in the process.

• • •

Jessie looked over the crowd, for the first time wishing it wasn't quite so big. Maybe she should have kept the club closed this week, just to be safe. She was relatively sure Tony would go by what he'd overheard in the cellar, especially since she'd reinforced that afterward. But there was always the chance that he'd try to call her bluff.

They had their escape route in place, and an exit strategy that shouldn't fail. She grabbed a tumbler that Joe had just filled and took a sip. She didn't drink much, but she needed something tonight. Her nerves were shot. Joe cocked an eyebrow and filled another glass for the couple who was waiting.

Maude sashayed over to her and slipped onto the stool next to hers. Jessie had no idea how the woman moved like that, almost like her feet weren't touching the floor at all.

"Honey, I've been waiting for you to show all night," Maude said, slapping her left hand down on the counter in front of Jessie. "Take a gander at that shiny handcuff, will you?"

"Oh Maude! It's beautiful," Jessie said, grabbing Maude's hand so she could see the ring better. "Who proposed?"

"Tommy Gallagher."

"The tailor from down the street?"

Maude nodded, a faint blush staining her cheeks, and Jessie smiled. Her friend looked genuinely happy. Jessie was a bit surprised. Maude had never seemed the type to want to settle down with one man, but Jessie supposed that the right man could make a woman change her mind. After all, one had almost changed hers.

Jessie shied away from that thought and threw her arms

around her friend, giving her a hug. "I'm so happy for you. That's wonderful news."

"Thank you, Jessie. That means so much to me. I was afraid you might be upset…"

"Why would I be upset?"

"Well, Tommy said he doesn't care if I keep singing, but I think he'd rather I didn't. Singin' in a speakeasy…well, I keep strange hours and since Tommy works all day, we wouldn't get to see each other much if I was here all night."

Jessie reached over and grabbed her friend's hand. "Don't you worry about it another second. I can always take over if I need to and besides, I'm not sure how much longer I'll keep this place going, anyhow."

"Jessie! You're not thinking of closing down?"

Jessie shrugged. "I never meant to keep this joint open long. With the Feds always sniffing around and now Willie poking his nose in, too, it seems like it might be a good time to bow out."

Maude's sharp eyes looked her over. "And what about your handsome Mr. Solomon?"

"He's not *my* anything."

"You could have fooled me, ducky."

Before Jessie could respond, a sudden flash of darkness drew her attention to the entrance tunnel. Another lamp was extinguished and a collective gasp of the suddenly panicked crowd had Jessie jumping to her feet, her pulse thundering in her ears. Raid!

She'd been stupid, so stupid! He *had* betrayed her. She should have kept the club closed. Damn it all!

There was no time to kick herself. She shoved aside her roiling emotions and focused past her heartache and fear to what was immediately important. Jessie ducked under the makeshift bar, helping Joe pull the set of shelves across the alcove where they stashed the liquor before turning to help get the bar down and stacked against the wall. When they were done, the bar area looked like a pile of old doors rotting next to a set of old storage shelves laden with years' worth of old junk.

The club was almost entirely dark now. The band members had led most of the patrons out through the tunnels toward the Dalton Street exit. But they weren't quick enough. The sound of a dozen pairs of boots stomping down the entrance tunnel had Jessie's heart pounding in her throat.

"This way!" she yelled, grabbing Maude's hand and waving to Joe. They ran for her office, slamming the door just as the first agent burst through the tunnel. Jessie turned the key, though she knew that wouldn't keep them out for long.

"Joe, help me," she said, running to the bookcase.

Together, they shoved it aside. Someone pounded on the door and the trio quickly slipped into the tunnel beyond the secret door. Joe closed it behind them, securing it with a thick plank of wood.

They took a deep breath, leaning against the wall and panting.

"Will they find us here?" Maude asked.

"I don't think so," Jessie said. "The only way into this tunnel is through the cellar in the shop. And I don't think they were watching the shop."

She and Joe exchanged a look. Jessie had no idea whether or not the cellar tunnel was safe. Tony knew where it was. He could easily lead the Feds down. Just like he'd led them to her speakeasy tonight.

A lump formed in her throat, but she tried to swallow past it, trying to ignore the pain lancing through her heart at his betrayal.

"I'm going to check out the cellar. If it's clear, we can go up the back stairs into my apartment and wait until morning. They can't arrest us for being in my own home."

Maude nodded and Jessie crept to the foot of the stairs, listening carefully. She didn't hear anything so she quietly ascended the stairs and slowly pushed open the trapdoor, just wide enough so she could see out.

The cellar was dark and deserted. "Come on," she whispered to her friends.

They followed her through the cellar to the back staircase, and up into her apartment. Jessie immediately went to the window. In the distance she could see flashing red lights, heard the distant wail of the sirens. But the majority of them weren't in the direction of Barker Street. They were over near the Dalton Street area. Where all her patrons had been led.

Jessie put her hand over her mouth, pain rolling through her in waves at the magnitude of his betrayal. He hadn't just taken her down. He'd taken down everyone in her club. She refused to cry in front of Maude and Joe. But then she looked at the street below her window and had to shove her fist in her mouth to keep from crying out, in pain or fury, she wasn't sure. She turned her back, shutting out the sight of a lone man, his hands shoved in his pockets, standing across the street watching her window.

She wanted to rush down there, rail at him, hit him, ask him if he'd done this. Ask him why.

Instead, she leaned against the wall, slid to the floor, and let the tears come.

Chapter Eighteen

Jessie didn't want to look up when the door opened. She knew who it was. "We're closed," she said, keeping her back to him. Why hadn't she locked the door?

"Jessie," Tony said.

She didn't answer him. She didn't need to. Instead, she hefted the tray of meat from under the counter and took it into the back. He followed.

Jessie stopped at the large refrigerator and Tony opened the door before she could do it herself. She paused long enough to glare at him before marching past him into the icebox. She dropped the tray down on a rack and pushed past him on her way out.

"I've got nothing to say to you."

He grabbed her arm, forcing her to turn and look at him. "I did it for your own good."

"You have got to be kidding me. My own good? Don't pretend you did what you did for anyone other than yourself."

"You were getting in too deep and you know it! It was bad enough when it was just the Feds, but if Willie was sending one of his top guys in here, then things were about to go really wrong, fast."

"You have no idea what you're talking about! Mario came in here because he likes to torture me. I had Willie handled. Another month and he would have been out of my hair."

"You had Willie handled?" he shouted. "No one *handles* Willie. You were in over your head and you know it! Jameson shutting you down was the best way to get you out of this mess without you having to pick sides. You can get out of the game without Willie thinking you hooked up with the Feds, and Jameson gets his arrests and will have no further reason to harass you. It was the best way!"

Jessie tried to brush him off but Tony wouldn't let her go. She sucked in several deep breaths, trying to control her rising panic. Part of her wanted nothing more than to throw herself in his arms and let him make everything all right. The other part just wanted to deck him.

"You're a fool if you believe that. Do you really think Willie will stop sniffing around because my club got raided? Do you think Jameson is just going to let me go? You didn't help me, you just put the last nail in my coffin!"

Her heart pounded so hard against her ribcage it hurt and she couldn't blink back the tears that clouded her vision.

"Jessie," Tony said, pulling her into his arms. "Baby, that's not true. I know it doesn't seem like it right now, but this is for the best, I promise you. I can help you."

She shook her head, letting him hold her for half a second before pushing out of his embrace. "Help me?" She laughed, though it sounded more like a sob. She knew she was on the verge of hysteria and tried desperately to rein herself in. "You can't help me, Tony. You've only made things worse."

"Jessie…"

"Why don't you go back to your Fed buddies? Or are they waiting outside? Did you just come in here to lead me out to them? Offer me up on a silver platter so you could get your precious career back?"

Tony's face paled, his jaw clenched. "They aren't my friends."

"But you *are* working for them."

He shoved his hands in his pockets, his body rigid. "I was. I'm not now."

She shook her head in disgust and backed another step away from him.

"I didn't know you, Jessie. I was hired to find the Phoenix. That was it."

"You used me."

"I never meant to."

She snorted and crossed her arms. "Really?"

He sighed and looked away, his eyes roaming around the room before coming back to rest on her. "I didn't mean…" He let out another exasperated sigh and raked his hands through his hair. "I just thought I could get some information on the Phoenix, a criminal. That was all. I didn't know how involved you were. I never thought…"

"Well, now you know." Jessie shook her head. She wasn't being entirely fair. She'd known from the start what he was up to and she'd been in danger long before he'd come along. But he'd definitely made it worse.

"No," he said, "I don't know. I still don't know what's going on. I know you are involved, heavily. And in Jameson's eyes, that makes you as much a criminal as the Phoenix. But that doesn't mean it's too late for you. Jameson will cut you a deal. Tell him what he wants to know and he'll go easy on you. I made sure he'd get you a good deal before I agreed to anything."

"You need to leave."

"Jessie, just let me explain. We don't have much time. You need to listen."

"There's nothing to explain. I understand perfectly. You

wanted the Phoenix and you thought you could romance the information you wanted out of me. It didn't work. End of story. Now you need to leave. I'd rather not have an audience when they haul me out of here in cuffs."

Tony flinched, but he stood his ground. "All you have to do is talk. Give Jameson what he wants. If you give him the Phoenix, Willie, everything, you might even walk."

"Get out."

"Damn it, Jessica! Why are you being so stubborn?"

Jessie sucked in a deep breath through her nose, trying desperately not to cry. The Feds were probably waiting outside to arrest her. And if they didn't get her, Willie would. His goons were watching her every move. They had to have seen Tony come into the shop and he'd been inside far too long. They'd think she was talking.

"Tony, please. Just leave."

"I'm not going until you tell me what's going on. This is more than you being mad at me. What's got you spooked?"

Jessie froze at a noise from the front of the shop. "Did you hear something?"

Tony listened. "I'm not sure."

"You've got to go," she said, pushing him toward the door, her panic overriding everything else. "Willie's guys have been watching my place. They know you are involved with the Feds. They think I'm feeding you info. If they see you here, I'm dead."

"Jessie. Jessie!" Tony said, breaking away from her and taking her face in his hands to make her listen. "I can help you. If you agree to testify, the Feds will protect you. You've just got to tell them what you know about the Phoenix. Make it up if you have to, as long as you give them *something* real. Something, anything. The location of your gin stash. Give them *something* and they'll agree to protect you from Willie and anyone else."

A laugh burbled up from Jessie's throat. She was losing her grip and slipping into hysteria. *What a joke.* Sure. If she wanted to keep Willie from killing her, all she had to do was turn herself in to the damn Feds. That would work out great.

"Jessie…"

Tony reached for her again, but Jessie backed away from him. "Leave. Please. Before it's too late."

Tony opened his mouth to argue again but was interrupted by the sound of a huge crash and glass shattering.

"Oh, no," Jessie breathed, terror clawing at her throat. She ran toward the noise in the front of the shop.

She pushed through the swinging door that led to the front. Tony yelled, "No!" and pulled her back as a wall of heat and flying glass hit her, throwing her backward. She crashed into a rolling cart of shelves. Flames seared her from her burning apron and she screamed.

Tony grabbed her, yanking the apron over her head and beating at the flames.

"Are you okay?"

Jessie nodded. Her arm was singed and cut from the glass, and she was bruised and battered, but she didn't think it was too bad.

Flames were everywhere, smoke filling the shop and flowing beneath the door into the back room. Tony grabbed Jessie and pulled her with him as he ran. They burst out of the back door and gunshots rang out. Tony yanked Jessie down into a squat and shoved her back through the door. Tires squealed as the car peeled off down the street. Tony slammed it shut and ran his hands over her.

"Are you hit? Are you okay?"

Jessie shook her head. "I don't know. I think I'm fine." She coughed. The smoke was growing so thick she couldn't see the ceiling anymore. Fire licked at the door, closing them off from the front of the shop.

"We're trapped," Tony said, pulling her into his arms. His eyes searched around the room. She could feel his heart pounding against her back.

"No, we aren't." She lunged away from him.

"Jessie!"

"Follow me!" She crawled to the trapdoor and levered it up.

Tony followed her without further questions. Jessie ran down the steps into the blessed coolness of the cellar. Tony pulled the door shut behind him and they were sealed in the darkness.

"Jessie?"

"I'm here," she called. She reached for him, her fingers closing on his outstretched hand as he slowly made his way down the stairs.

"We can't go to your storeroom. The stone might prevent the fire from spreading down here, but just in case, a room full of liquor really wouldn't be the best place to wait."

"No kidding."

"Then where are we going?"

Jessie didn't answer, just pulled him along the path she knew so well. She didn't need a light to tell her where she was. When they reached the end of the tunnel, she ran her fingers along the wall until she found the latch that would open the door into her office. Once inside, she felt her way to her desk and yanked open the bottom drawer where she always kept a spare flashlight.

She flicked it on and held it up high enough that she could see Tony's face, being careful not to shine it right in his eyes. He stared at her, his face expressionless. "Where the hell are we?"

"The Red Phoenix."

He quickly glanced around the office, then back at her. She couldn't read his expression and was glad of it. She wasn't sure she wanted to know what was going on behind those deep, dark eyes of his.

She turned her back on him and yanked open another desk drawer. She tossed everything out of it, then reached in the back to unlatch the secret drawer beneath the false bottom. Tony watched in silence. She ignored him, but her heart ached at the thought of what he might be thinking of her.

Once she accessed the secret compartment, she grabbed a small stack of cash and the little revolver she'd purchased when she'd opened the speakeasy. She'd wanted to be able to defend herself if the need ever arose. No time like the present, that was for sure.

She risked another glance at Tony.

He arched an eyebrow. "We need to talk."

Jessie snorted. Understatement of the year.

Tony grabbed her uninjured arm and took the gun from her hand. "Give that to me."

She glared at him and opened her mouth to argue but he stopped her. "You can't go out there armed. If the Feds catch you and you've got a gun on you…"

Jessie seethed, but knew he had a point.

"Besides, I'm probably a better shot than you. If Willie is still out there, we need every bullet to count."

"Fine. Let's go," she said, leading the way into the main club. The rooms were built of thick stone, so she was relatively sure they were safe from the fire above, but she didn't want to test her theory. And she didn't want to be trapped in the chambers if Willie's men decided to come looking for them.

Tony followed her through the pitch-dark tunnel, the beam of her flashlight flickering eerily off the walls and furniture. Keeping the club in complete darkness when it wasn't open was one of her safety precautions. If anyone ever managed to get inside, she didn't want to leave the lights on to show them the way. The hope was that any intruders would

just get lost in the other passages without ever stumbling into
The Red Phoenix.

Finally, they reached an outer tunnel that was rarely used
because it led to an exit very close to the shop. Under normal
circumstances, using such a close exit would be avoided, but
this time Jessie needed to see what was happening with her
shop and she didn't want to have to run several blocks to do it.

They reached the door that led to the outside. Jessie pulled
back the eye portal panel and took a quick look outside. The
alleyway beyond the door was dark and empty and she pushed
open the door, slipping into the alley. She prayed that Willie
didn't have anyone watching the shop. They had a decent shot
since they knew she and Tony had both been inside when it
had been firebombed. And she was the only one who knew
about the tunnel leading from the shop into the speakeasy.

She stepped around the corner and got her first glimpse.
Her shop. The front of the building was gone, destroyed in
the explosion. The flames were spreading to the upper floors,
pushing out the windows as they climbed. Her knees gave out
as a wave of despair washed over her and she slumped to the
ground. Her father's shop, the reason she'd been doing all of
this in the first place, was gone.

The orange haze made the night sky glow. It would have
been pretty if it hadn't been her heart and soul going up in
flames. The wind blew in their direction, bringing the acrid
scent of smoke and flame. In a few moments, the shop would
be nothing more than a pile of cinders. The last connection
she had to her father would be gone. And she'd be completely
alone in the world.

Yes, her father had been gone awhile. But somehow, being
there in his shop had made his loss a little more bearable.
Like some part of him was still there. Still with her. That shop
was the only home she'd known. The only place she'd known
happiness. Love. Whenever she missed her father, all she'd had

to do was look around. She could see his touch everywhere. Every nook and cranny held some memory of him.

The first floor ceiling caved in to where the main shop area had been, raining sparks and fanning the flames anew. Overwhelming desolation rose up to choke her and she hunched over, trying to huddle against the pain. It was like losing him all over again. She couldn't do this. It was too much. She couldn't bear any more. She moaned, the sound erupting from her lips like the keening of a wounded animal. Finally, the tears pushed past the lump in her throat and she let them come.

"Jessie." Tony sat beside her and pulled her onto his lap and into his arms, holding her while she sobbed.

He rocked her, his hand tangling in her hair as he pressed her head to his chest, his lips brushing her forehead, kissing the top of her head. He held her, caressed her, murmured soothing nonsense in her ear until she cried herself out and just lay against him, exhausted.

"You've got to let me help you," he said cautiously. "I know you don't want to do this, but you've got to give up any information you've got on the Phoenix and the club. There's no reason to protect anyone now. You need to worry about your own safety. Give up whatever you've got, the location of the operation, *anything*, and the Feds will put you under protective custody. You'll be safe—from Willie and…anyone else who might mean you harm."

Jessie let out a bark of laughter.

"You think they'll protect me? Sure, until I give them everything I've got to bargain with and then they'll hang me out to rot."

"Jessie, I promise you, I'll make sure you are protected. I'd never let anything happen to you. But my hands are tied if you don't give up…"

"Who? The Phoenix? There *is* no Phoenix!"

Tony stiffened, his face going rigid, his eyes unreadable. She pushed away from him, at the end of her rope.

"Don't you get it? *I* am the Phoenix. It's *my* club. *I* run it. *I'm* the boss. There *is* no one else."

Tony stood and stared at her. His face was pale but not surprised. He already knew. Had probably known for a while now.

"There is no Phoenix. And there is no operation. I wasn't lying or hiding anything. I've told the Feds that a hundred times. I'm not making the stuff. I never needed to. My father made gin his whole life. You saw the cellar, and that was only a portion of what there is. I was just selling it so I could pay off my father's debt to Willie. Then that would have been it for The Red Phoenix. So I've got nothing left to bargain for my safety. If I go to the Feds, they'll arrest me for bootlegging. If I stay put, Willie will bump me off. My life is over any way you look at."

Tony was breathing as though he'd run twenty miles, his nostrils flaring and his eyes wide. Jessie just watched him and the fight drained out of her. There was nowhere to run. Nowhere to hide. And she'd lost Tony, too. He'd betrayed her, turned her over to Jameson to save his sorry career. There wasn't anything left to fight for.

"Leave me, Tony. Leave me in peace. You've done enough damage for one day."

Tony shook his head once and hauled her into his arms, his lips pressing against hers. Jessie struggled against him, shoving him away. Her depression evaporated, replaced by a fury so great she could scarcely breathe. She reached back and let her arm swing, her palm connecting with Tony's face. The impact rang through the alley and shuddered up her arm, leaving an ache to match the one in her heart.

"Don't ever touch me again," she whispered, too furious and soul-sick to force the words louder.

Boots crunched on the gravel as the officers came running. Jessie backed away from Tony though her gaze remained riveted on him.

"Put your hands where I can see them!"

"Jameson, wait…" Tony said, moving to stand in front of Jessie.

"Get out of the way, Solomon, unless you want to be arrested along with her."

Jessie stood and held out her hands. Tony didn't move; he didn't try to stop the officer who came over to cuff her. Jessie ignored Jameson, ignored the officer, though she cried out when he tried to wrench her arm behind her back. She just watched Tony.

His hands were balled into fists at his side, the vein in his forehead jumping. "Jameson," he ground out through gritted teeth. "You can't arrest her. She needs to be taken to the hospital. She was hurt in the explosion."

Jameson didn't look concerned in the slightest. "She'll be taken care of, don't worry."

The officer started to lead Jessie away but Tony reached out and took her arm. "I'm going with her."

Jameson's face darkened and he clamped a hand on Tony's shoulder. "You've done good work, Solomon. Now get out of the way."

Jessie looked up at Tony, their eyes locked. He took half a step toward her but she shook her head.

It was over. The Feds had her. Tony had betrayed her. Her shop was gone. Let it be done. She turned her back on Tony and let the officer lead her away.

Chapter Nineteen

Tony stood outside Jessie's hospital room until his legs started going numb. The guard posted outside her door gave him a few curious looks, but for the most part ignored him.

He'd been waiting since they'd brought her in hours ago, with nothing to do but run through every detail of the last several weeks in his mind. He'd been a damn fool. Yes, Jessie hadn't been totally honest with him, but she'd had her reasons. She was nothing like Lucille. Nothing. Her lies, her evasiveness, even her involvement in the club, had all been for the good of others. There wasn't an evil bone in her body. She would never have betrayed him as Lucille did.

No. *He* was the one who'd betrayed her. He'd known deep down that she was an innocent, that whatever she was mixed up in, it was for a good reason. And he'd turned her in anyway. He'd been so afraid of repeating past mistakes that he'd made a whole slew of new ones. Worse mistakes. Yes, the evidence had pointed to her being dirty. But his gut had told him the truth. But he'd been so afraid to screw up again he'd given up the woman he…he loved.

He sank to his haunches, leaning against the wall and letting his elbows rest on his knees, his head hanging. He didn't care what she'd done, what sorts of lies she'd told. Despite all of it, he loved her. Loved her so much her absence was like a gaping hole in his shredded heart. She might be just on the other side of the wall, but she may as well have been thousands of miles away.

He'd lost her. He knew it. If he'd trusted his instincts, if he'd tried harder to gain her trust, find out what was really going on, or hell, even given her the chance to tell him her side of the story before he'd given her up to Jameson, then maybe he'd have a chance.

But he'd done none of those things. He'd let his fear and his past get in the way. And the price was Jessie.

Finally, Tony sighed and straightened up. She hated him. He knew that. He'd made a mess of things and she'd probably never forgive him. If she didn't, he'd have to live with that. But he wanted her to know all the details before he walked out of her life for good. She deserved so much more, but he could give her that much at least.

He pushed her door open and let it close quietly behind him. She wasn't asleep. She lay in the bed, looking somehow smaller than she had before. Her arm was wrapped up to the elbow. He pulled a chair over and sat by her bed. She kept her attention fixed on the window, on the rain that ran in tiny rivulets down the panes.

"Jessie?"

She didn't answer.

Tony wracked his brain, not knowing how to start. How do you apologize for destroying someone's life? "The doctors said your arm should heal well. You'll get out of here soon."

She gave a mirthless laugh. "Yes, but to go where? Home?" She finally looked at him and the haunted sadness in her eyes carved a hole in his heart. She looked back out the window. "I don't even have a home to go to."

"Jessie…"

A quiet sigh escaped her. "What do you want, Tony?"

"To talk."

"I think everything that needed to be said has been said. Let's just leave each other in peace."

Tony shook his head. "You don't know. I need you to understand why…"

She looked at him again, her eyes huge and bright in her pale face. "I don't need to know why. It doesn't matter."

He wanted to gather her to him and just hold her.

"Yes, it does. I didn't do this to hurt you, Jessie. I didn't set out to destroy your life."

"Didn't you? You walked into my shop with the express purpose of getting as close to me as possible, romantically, if necessary, in order to get information on the Phoenix so you could arrest him and shut down his speakeasy. Right?"

Tony leaned forward, resting his elbows on his knees. "Yes," he said, weariness coating the word.

"Then you'll excuse me if I don't believe you didn't mean to destroy me, when that is exactly what you set out to do, by any means necessary. Only it wasn't enough for you to just destroy my life. You had to destroy my heart, too."

"I never wanted to hurt you, Jessie," Tony said, nearly choking on his regret. "I'm sorry. I truly am."

Jessie was silent for a moment. "You could have stopped it."

"Yes. But I was too afraid of making another mistake."

Jessie was quiet for a moment, then let out a small sigh. "Like the one that cost your partner his life?"

Tony's gaze shot to hers, shock thrumming through him. "You know about that?"

She nodded. "Mario gave me a newspaper clipping, warned me not to trust you."

Tony closed his eyes and rubbed a hand over his face. "That's what was in the envelope he gave you."

Jessie's eyes widened, but only slightly. Tony supposed with everything else she'd found out, knowing he'd seen that exchange wasn't particularly shocking.

"What did you give him?"

Jessie closed her eyes and leaned back against her pillow. "My father owed Willie money and when he died, Willie expected me to pay off the debt. I was late with a payment, so Mario came to collect."

Tony let out a long breath. "Why didn't you tell me?"

Jessie didn't answer that, but then she didn't need to. Tony knew exactly why she hadn't confided in him.

"He also warned me that they'd be watching in case I decided to switch sides and join you," she said, her voice small, quiet.

"Which is why they bombed your shop."

Jessie shrugged, grimacing when the movement pulled on her arm. "Who knows? Maybe they thought I was too close to you. Maybe they wanted to send a message to the Phoenix. Maybe they just thought I was overcharging for steaks. It doesn't really matter. My shop is gone."

Tony leaned over and took her hand, relief flooding him when she allowed it. "I'm sorry, Jessie. For all of it."

She looked at him, those big blue eyes he loved finally meeting his. He could drown in those eyes. They would haunt his dreams for the rest of his life. He could only pray that someday the happy spark he loved so much would return. All he knew for sure was that he would never, ever again be responsible for an ounce of pain marring their lovely depths. He'd die first.

"Well, isn't this cozy?"

Jameson pushed through the door and came around to the other side of Jessie's bed. Jessie removed her hand from

Tony's, pulling her blankets up like they'd be added protection against the agent staring her down.

"Really, Miss Harlan, you must be an incredibly forgiving person. I'm impressed."

"What do you mean?" she asked.

"Well, I know if I were in your shoes, I wouldn't be speaking to the man who brought me down, let alone lying there holding his hand."

"Jameson, enough. Let her be."

Jameson cocked an eyebrow. "Didn't you come to gloat?" he asked Tony. "You should be proud. A whole team of my agents couldn't make a crack in that façade she had up. Yet you brought down the whole operation in just under three months. It's impressive, truly. I might even recommend you get your job back on the force. They were too hasty letting you go after that little mess with your partner."

Tony stood and took a step in Jameson's direction, not caring what the consequences would be if he decked the man. Jessie's voice stopped him.

"What was impressive?"

Jameson turned a sneering smile on Jessie. "Miss Harlan, it is my very great pleasure to inform you that you'll be brought up on charges of racketeering, obstruction of justice, the illegal ownership and sale of alcohol, and any other charges we can make stick in conjunction with your running of the speakeasy called The Red Phoenix."

Jessie breathed slowly in and out, but her face was as white as the sheets she laid on. "You don't have any proof of any of that."

"What? Didn't he tell you?"

"Tell me what?" Jessie bit out, her eyes darting back and forth between Jameson and Tony.

"Jameson," Tony warned.

Jameson ignored him. "We've got all the evidence we

need to put you away for a very long time. Photographs of your private stores, not to mention all the confiscated hooch we found at the club, the location of the speakeasy, all the contents of your office, and photographs of you accepting payoffs from Mario Russo, a well-known associate of Willie the Weasel. All courtesy of Mr. Solomon here."

Jessie looked at Tony, her eyes wide, her tears making them liquid pools of sapphire.

"Now," Jameson continued, though Jessie kept her eyes on Tony, "if you'd like to be cooperative, we might be able to make a deal."

Jameson grasped the end of her bed and leaned over, startling her into looking at him. "Give us the Phoenix and you might just get out of prison before all that pretty hair of yours turns gray."

Jessie's forehead crinkled in confusion and her gaze flicked to Tony. "But…"

Tony grabbed Jameson's arm and pulled him away from her bed. "That's enough, Jameson. You've said what you wanted to say. You can't expect her to make a decision like that right away."

Jameson glared at Tony, but finally nodded. "Fine then. Twenty-four hours, Miss Harlan. When you decide who's going to prison, you let me know."

He shook Tony's hand off his arm and marched from the room.

Tony went back to the side of the bed, Jessie's round eyes following him the whole time. He stared down at her. Down at this woman who would own his heart and soul until the day he died.

"I know I've made a mess of things, Jessie. I can't fix everything. But I'll do what I can to make this right. I swear it to you."

He leaned down and kissed her forehead and then turned

and left her with tears streaming down her cheeks.

• • •

Tony went straight to his office and began pulling files and film from the safe where he'd stashed all his information on Jessie and the Phoenix. He'd told Jameson what he had on Jessie. But he hadn't turned any of it over yet and Jameson had been too stupid to insist.

For the first time, Tony was grateful for the rickety little woodburning stove that served to heat his office. He yanked open the door and began feeding the files into it, one at a time, making sure they were completely consumed. Then he tossed the photos he'd taken—of Jessie accepting the envelope from Russo, of the tunnels beneath the shop, of the cellar full of gin. All of it. Within minutes, every last piece of evidence he'd collected was destroyed.

Then he sat at his desk and waited for Jameson to show. He didn't have to wait long.

Chapter Twenty

Jessie sat on the edge of her hospital bed, frowning while Maude buckled her shoes. Her arm felt much better but it still ached a bit and Maude insisted on helping her.

She was about to tell Maude, for the fourth time, that she was capable of putting on her own shoes when the door suddenly burst open with such force that it slammed against the wall. Maude yelped and jumped back. Jessie would have dearly loved to follow suit, but she forced herself to stay put, even when Jameson stormed across the room and leaned down so he was right in her face.

"You might have fooled that jackass Solomon, but you don't fool me. I know you are involved in all this and I'm going to prove it, if it's the last thing I do."

Jessie's heart raced but she sat as straight as she could, trying not to let her anxiety show. She wouldn't give Jameson the satisfaction of seeing her cower. "I don't know what you're talking about."

"All the evidence is gone!"

"What do you mean? I thought you already had all the

evidence you needed."

"You want to sit there and play innocent, fine. I went to Solomon's office to collect everything he had on you, only now he claims that I *misunderstood*," he sneered, "that there never was any evidence. No photos, no files, no notes. Nothing!"

Jessie's breath caught in her throat with the sudden pounding of her heart. Was he saying what she thought he was saying? She quickly glanced at Maude, who was sitting in a chair clutching her pearls to her chest like a duchess about to have the vapors. Then she turned her attention back to Jameson.

"Agent Jameson, I really have no idea what you are talking about."

"You little bitch," he growled, leaning down, his arms on either side of Jessie so she couldn't move.

Maude screamed, but Jameson ignored her. Jessie's breaths were coming in short, frightened pants, terror at Jameson's rage squeezing her chest like a vise. Three nurses, a doctor, and the officer who'd been guarding the door all clustered around, but no one was sure what to do. After all, Jameson was a federal agent.

"You won't get away with this, you hear me?" His eyes bulged and Jessie shrank away from him despite her best intentions to remain stoic. "I'll be watching you. One slipup and you'll be mine." He straightened and turned to stomp from the room. "Let's go," he said to the officer at the door.

The cop glanced back at Jessie, confusion mirroring what Jessie was sure was on her own face, before he turned and followed Jameson.

As soon as he was gone, the medical staff clustered about Jessie, fussing and prodding at her, trying to make sure she was unharmed. She was grateful for their concern but she needed to get out of there now. If what Jameson had said was true, then Tony had made good on his promise to set things right. The thought eased the ache in her heart somewhat, but filled her with anxiety for him. Jameson was not going to let this go.

After assuring the doctor and nurses that she was fine, Jessie filled out her discharge papers and all but ran from the hospital, Maude close on her heels.

"Jessie, what was all that about?" Maude asked, huffing a bit as she hurried to keep up with Jessie.

"I think Tony might have just done something very stupid. Incredibly sweet," she said, her heart swelling with fear-tinged joy, "but very, very stupid."

They got to Maude's car, courtesy of her new fiancé, and slid inside. "Where to?" Maude asked, knowing without having to ask that they weren't going back to her place.

Jessie thought for a second. She had no idea what had really happened or where Tony might be. But she knew who would know. She gave Maude Tony's mother's address.

His mother opened the door before she had a chance to knock. "Saw you pull up," she said. "He's not here."

"What's happened, Mrs. Solomon?"

His mother held the door open and Jessie and Maude trailed inside, but Jessie was too anxious to sit.

"He was arrested," his mother said, getting right to the point.

"What?" Jessie whispered, sinking onto a chair. "Why?"

"For obstruction of justice."

Jessie shook her head, a lump forming in her throat. "I don't understand."

Mrs. Solomon sighed and sat down. "It's fairly easy. He loves you."

Jessie's head jerked up. "But he…he didn't…what did he do?"

Mrs. Solomon smiled. "Well, I expect he finally told that dumbbell Jameson what to go do with himself."

Jessie knew her mouth was hanging open like a carp, but she couldn't seem to process the abrupt turn her life had taken. Too many emotions warred within her. The love that she'd tried to deny bubbled up, her body fairly pulsing with it. But the doubts were still there, the little voice in the back of her head whispering that he wouldn't do such a thing, not for her, not after all the lies she'd told, the mistrust and betrayal between them. And yet...beneath it all was something she hadn't felt in a very long time. A glimmer of hope.

"Jameson said Tony told him there was no evidence, that he didn't have anything on me. But he did. Photos, files. I know he did."

Mrs. Solomon sat forward and took Jessie's hands. "If he did, then I'd guess they are ash at the bottom of his fireplace about now."

Jessie closed her eyes and let her head hang, the enormity of what Tony had done for her hitting her like a hundred pound sack of flour. Mrs. Solomon squeezed her hands and Jessie looked back up at her.

She studied Jessie's face, looked deep into her eyes. "Anthony told me what happened, what he did. I know he hurt you. But...my son has had a hard time of it. He made a mistake that he's spent years trying to make up for. No one will let him forget it, least of all himself. And he worries too much about me. But he's a good man. Whatever he's done, it's because he thought he was doing the right thing. Never forget that."

Jessie nodded, her throat closing around the tears that threatened, once again, to fall.

Mrs. Solomon watched her for a moment. "You must be something special for my boy to give up everything he's worked for."

Jessie shook her head. "I'm nothing, no one. I don't want him to ruin his life for me. I don't know why he'd do this."

Maude snorted. "The man just went to prison for you. I'd call that love."

Mrs. Solomon laughed. "I'd have to agree."

The small spark of hope flamed brighter in Jessie's heart and she ducked her head, trying to sort through all the emotions roiling through her. "Do you know where they've taken him?"

Mrs. Solomon pushed herself out of her chair and retrieved a slip of paper off the counter.

"Don't tell him I gave it to you," she said with a wink.

Jessie took the paper and Mrs. Solomon enveloped her in a hug. "Give him a chance, *hmm*?"

Jessie gave her a tremulous smile, her heart filling with warmth, and nodded.

She and Maude drove in silence to the jailhouse. Jessie's head spun. The magnitude of what Tony had done for her finally sank in as she saw the bars and guards crawling all over the place.

Maude pulled the car over in front of the building and parked. "I'll wait for you out here."

Jessie nodded, but didn't make a move to get out. Her heart thundered in her chest.

"What are you waiting for?" Maude asked.

"I don't know…I'm not even sure what to say to him. He betrayed me, destroyed everything…"

"And then refused to turn you over and got thrown in jail for it. I think he's more than made up for it."

Jessie shook her head, regret for her own actions filling her. She'd felt justified at the time, but now… "What if he doesn't want to see me? He's in that place because of me, and I was horrible to him."

"You had every right to be. I'm sure he understands. Now get in there."

Jessie took a deep breath, shoving her emotions back

until she had time to deal with them, and opened the car door. She let her hope propel her forward, kept the image of his face the last time she'd seen him in her mind.

She was afraid it might be hard to get in to see him, afraid maybe Jameson had put some restrictions or something in place to prevent it. But the sergeant in charge had her sign in and led her to a visiting area. Tony wasn't exactly seen as a high priority, dangerous criminal, so he would be allowed to see her without a pane of glass between them. But even so, when they led him out he was dressed in prison garb and had his hands cuffed in front of him.

Jessie froze at the sight of him, her blood pounding so furiously through her veins that it nearly deafened her. He stood there, his eyes crinkled with confusion, shame maybe... but that same glow of hope that flared in her breast shone from his face.

She hadn't been sure what she'd say or do when she saw him, but it turned out she didn't have time to think about it. As soon as he was close enough to touch she wrapped her arms around him and buried her face in his chest.

He hesitated only a second and then raised his arms, allowing her to slip under them so he could hold her.

"What are you doing here?" he asked, kissing the top of her head.

"What are *you* doing here?" she retorted. "What on earth were you thinking? Have you completely lost your marbles?"

He smiled down at her and the expression made her toes tingle. "I think I might have."

She smiled back but shook her head. "Why did you..."

His arms tightened around her, his eyes flashing a warning at her. She suddenly remembered where they were.

"You're innocent," he said simply. "The Phoenix is the one who ran the club. He's the one Jameson needs to be going after. Not you."

Jessie looked up at him in surprise. Tony just smiled and gave her a small wink. She huddled back against his chest to hide her smile. It was sort of perfect, she supposed. Pin it all on the Phoenix. It would get them both off the hook and it wasn't really a lie. They'd just keep the part about her being the Phoenix out of it.

Tony led her over to a bench and they sat as close together as they could, their heads bowed together so they could speak with some semblance of privacy, though a guard hovered nearby.

"I think you should tell Jameson what you know," Tony said, his eyes quickly glancing at the guard and then back again.

Realization dawned on Jessie. That's why it had been so easy getting in to see him. Jameson had probably hoped she'd visit, that they'd talk and maybe let something incriminating slip.

"If you think that would be best," Jessie answered.

Tony nodded. "With the club compromised, especially since Willie's guys burned your shop, the Phoenix has probably pulled out, anyway. Tell Jameson what you can, turn over everything related to the Phoenix that you've got, prove that you're willing to cooperate, and Jameson will have to leave you alone. After all, you aren't the Phoenix. You can't be held responsible for his actions, and if you spill what you know, well then…there's not a lot more Jameson can expect from you."

"I suppose you're right," Jessie said.

Tony leaned in closer, spoke in hardly more than a whisper. "Make a deal. Show him everything you can in exchange for immunity. He'll take it."

Jessie nodded, then looked up into Tony's eyes. "Why?"

He knew she wasn't talking about Jameson anymore. "I owed you."

"No. You didn't. Not this," she said, running her hand

down his prison duds.

He brought his cuffed hands up and caught her hand, keeping it pressed against his chest. "I made a mistake. I'm just glad this was one I could fix."

"Time's up," the guard said.

Jessie looked at Tony in sudden panic. "How long will you be in here?"

He shrugged. "Until Jameson decides I've been punished enough, I suppose. I'm not sure."

Jessie's stomach dropped, a sudden fear pouring through her that if she walked away now, she'd never see him again. She shook her head. "No, this isn't fair."

He chuckled. "Life isn't fair, baby."

"Come on," the guard said, resting his hand on his nightstick.

Tony leaned down swiftly, before Jessie or the guard could protest, and kissed her. She grabbed his face, keeping him pressed to her lips.

"Enough of that!" the guard shouted, pulling his nutcracker and grabbing Tony by the back of the collar. "Don't make me use this on you!" he said, shoving the nightstick under Tony's chin.

Jessie gasped and clapped her hands over her mouth, but Tony just smiled at her. "Drop me a line every now and then."

Before Jessie could respond, the guard hauled Tony off. Jessie watched until she couldn't see him anymore and then she marched out of the jailhouse and slid into Maude's car.

"So, how did it go?"

Jessie shook her head. "That man is a stubborn, stupid fool."

"And you're goofy over him," Maude said, grinning.

"Yeah." Jessie laughed and shook her head again. "Just my luck."

"Well, where to now?"

"The federal building. Agent Jameson and I need to have a chat."

Chapter Twenty-One

Jameson didn't keep her waiting. When she was shown into his office, he sat behind his desk with his fingers steepled together like some theatrical villain, and a smug expression that Jessie desperately longed to knock off his face.

"Ready to talk?"

Jessie nodded.

"I thought you might be. Have a seat."

Jessie perched on the edge of the chair in front of the desk. "I've got a few conditions."

"You're in no position to be making conditions."

"On the contrary, Agent Jameson, I think you're the one who is in no position to be quibbling."

Jameson frowned darkly at her, but Jessie pressed on. "You've spent a great deal of money trying to pinch the Phoenix. Broken a few laws along the way. And all you've gotten for your trouble is one ex-detective who says he doesn't know anything. I can't imagine your superiors are very happy about that. I've got information that will make all your troubles go away. I think that's worth something."

Jameson's scowl deepened, but he didn't refute any of it. "So, what are your conditions?"

Jessie bit back the grin. No need to rub it in. "Immunity. For myself and Tony."

"No," Jameson nearly growled. "For Solomon, no. For you…I'll consider it. Depending on what you can deliver."

"I'll tell you everything I know about the Phoenix."

Jameson's scowl lessened. "I want the Phoenix himself."

Jessie shook her head. "I can't give you the man. He's long gone."

Jameson sat back with a huff. "Then what can you give me that's valuable enough to buy your immunity?"

"Everything else. I can take you inside the club, show you all the hidden nooks and crannies. His stock of liquor. I know my way around the network of tunnels. I can show you which ones he used." Jessie took a deep breath. This one was going to hurt. "And I've got his files. Including the information that will give you access to the bank account that financed the club."

Now Jameson was interested. He tried to play it cool, but Jessie knew the man was salivating. He might not be able to turn in the man himself, but if he could deliver all his liquor, his speakeasy, *and* his dough? That might just buy Jameson out of trouble.

She'd be sorry to see the money go. She'd squirreled away enough to last for a while after paying off Willie from her own account, but losing the lion's share of the club's account that would have meant security for her butcher shop would sting. Worth it though, to buy herself and Tony out of trouble. Can't run a shop from prison. And Jameson might balk on letting Tony go, but they both knew he couldn't keep him for long.

"Do we have a deal?" she asked.

"I don't know," he said, his brow furrowing in concentration. Poor man. Thinking that hard must have given him a headache.

"Playing hard to get, Agent Jameson?"

Jameson scowled at her. "I'm not sure how much this information is worth. We've seen the tunnels under your shop, and confiscated the liquor stores already."

"You only confiscated the ones you know about."

"There are more?"

Jessie smiled. "Much more."

Jameson let out a low whistle but still hesitated. Jessie's smile faded, her patience at an end. Enough was enough. "It's a good deal and you know it, Jameson."

He frowned at her, but finally he said, "Fine. You've got a deal. Your immunity—"

"And leniency for Tony, if you won't give him full immunity."

Jameson's face puckered like a sour persimmon, but he jerked his head in quick agreement. "For *all* the information you've got on the Phoenix. Including his real name."

Jessie had thought about that. Whether she should give the man a fictitious name or not. In the end, she just couldn't justify possibly having some poor schmuck with the same name being harassed by the good agent.

"I don't know his name."

"You really expect me to believe that?"

Jessie shrugged. "No one knew his name. I called him Phoenix. For all I know that *was* his real name. I've heard stranger."

Jameson shook his head.

"You'll have plenty of other goodies to turn in, Jameson. Don't fret."

"You better deliver."

"I will. But I want our deal witnessed and in writing before I show you anything."

"Fine."

"Well then," Jessie said, pushing out of her chair. "Meet

me at the butcher shop at nine tomorrow morning. And I'd appreciate it if you'd bring the papers with you."

Jameson nodded and Jessie let herself out of his office, feeling lighter than she had in quite a while, despite what she still had hanging over her head.

Jameson was at the butcher shop, bright and early, with nicely signed legal documents giving Jessie immunity in exchange for her turning over everything she had on the Phoenix. Jameson wasn't too impressed when Jessie took him down the trapdoor into the cellar. After all, as he said, he'd seen that bit before. Seen the cellar with its now empty shelves. But he hadn't seen what happened when the farthest shelf was pushed out of the way, opening into a vast chamber that was stocked to the ceiling with barrels of gin.

Jessie didn't bother to hide her smug smile. This whole mess had been nothing but a miserable pain and it was rather fun knowing how much she'd been able to conceal from the little weasel. Watching Jameson's mouth drop open was almost enough to make up for everything she was giving up. Almost.

"Your father made all this?"

Jessie shrugged. "Fiddled with it every day of his life, and his father did before him. More than they could ever drink. So it ended up down here until they needed it."

Jameson became a little less surly after that. Jessie took him down the tunnel that led to her office, where she turned over all the files. Jameson's eyes lit up like a five-year-old kid on Christmas morning. He didn't bother going through all the tunnels, though he sent his men to scope them out. He was too eager to get back to his office and show off all his new acquisitions.

"Well, Miss Harlan. It was a pleasure doing business with you but I sincerely hope we never see each other again."

"The feeling is mutual, Agent Jameson."

He gave her a cold smile and tucked the last file into a box.

"Jameson," she said, before he could leave. "About Tony…"

"No. Solomon can cool his heels for a few weeks. That's as *lenient* as I'll go. I might not be able to prove he destroyed evidence, but his gross misappropriation of funds while he was undercover is enough to earn him a little jail time."

Jessie bit her tongue to keep from saying something she might regret.

"Don't worry, Miss Harlan. Greaseballs like Solomon always slither their way out of trouble."

"You'll never be half the man that Tony is," she said, pushed to the breaking point.

But Jameson just smiled at her. "That is your opinion, Miss Harlan. Good-day."

Jessie was glad to see him walk out her door. If she never set eyes on him again, she'd be a very happy woman.

She slumped into her chair. She couldn't believe it was over. The speakeasy was gone. The booze was gone. The Feds were off her tail. Willie had done his worst and now that the rumor was spreading that both the Phoenix and his club were history, she didn't think she'd have any more problems with him. Especially since she'd made sure his last payment had made its way into his corrupt little pocket. With her father's debt paid off, Willie didn't have any reason to be interested in her.

She had insurance money, and the private stash she'd held back from the club's money that she'd turned over, so she could rebuild the shop. Could even improve on it. She laid her head on her arms and closed her eyes. Her life was her own again. But it wasn't complete yet…not without Tony.

Chapter Twenty-Two

Jessie grabbed another bucket of paint and lugged it into the main shop area. It was amazing what a couple of months had done for the place. The outside was completely rebuilt. They just needed to get the inside to match. The shop area had been finished first. The workmen only needed to finish up the living quarters upstairs and she'd be able to fully move back in.

Maude had kindly taken her in while the building had been rebuilt, but the second the walls had gone up, Jessie had hauled an old mattress up the stairs so she could sleep in her own place again. She longed for the day when it would be completely finished.

Even more than that, Jessie yearned to see Tony again. Since he'd been away, he'd written to her every week, without fail. But he refused to allow her to come visit. The one time she'd tried, she'd been turned away. She'd given him an earful for it in her letters, but he refused to budge. The man was infuriating. She just wanted to see him. She didn't care where that might be. But he'd insisted, and so she'd spent the last couple months pining for him.

She'd never pictured herself as the pining type, but she needed the man, plain and simple. It had been a blessing, perhaps, that they'd had the chance to get to know each other better through their letters without the heat of their attraction getting in the way. But it had been long enough and Jessie wanted her man.

The door opened, the brand-new bell tinkling a welcome to whoever had entered. Jessie turned to tell them she wasn't open for business yet, but the words stuck in her throat.

His broad shoulders filled the doorway, the sunlight gleaming off his black hair, his deep brown eyes creasing at the corners with the width of his smile.

Jessie squealed, a noise she had never made before in her entire life, dropped the brush she held in her hand, and launched herself at Tony. He laughed and caught her, supporting her weight so she could wrap her legs around his waist and her arms around his neck.

Her lips were on his, her hands fisted in his hair, before he could get a word out. He didn't seem to mind though. He kissed her until she had to wrench herself away to suck in a deep breath.

"You're here," she said, near breathless with joy.

"I'm here," he said, leaning in for another soul-altering kiss.

"Why didn't you tell me?" she asked, breaking away long enough to press a trail of kisses down his neck.

He kicked the door closed and carried her farther into the shop, placing her on the newly built counter. She kissed him again and again, and finally wrapped her arms around his neck so she could just hold him.

He stroked down her back, making quiet shushing sounds while he murmured the most beautiful nonsense in her ears. She didn't realize tears were slipping down her face until he kissed them from her cheeks.

"I missed you," she said, smiling up at him.

He laughed. "I noticed." He leaned down for a long, lingering kiss. "I missed you, too."

He untangled himself just enough so he could get a good look at her and Jessie suddenly remembered what she looked like.

"Oh horsefeathers! I'm a mess! Don't look at me like this." She covered her face with her hands, mortified beyond words.

Tony laughed again and pulled her hands away. "You are the most beautiful thing I have ever laid eyes on."

Jessie seriously doubted that. She'd been painting and in an effort to save her severely diminished wardrobe, had borrowed a pair of paint-splattered workman's overalls, and had covered her hair with a cloth.

"Show me around the new place," he said.

Jessie jumped off the counter and grabbed his hand, her heart near to bursting with happiness.

Tony took a step backward and stumbled, nearly jumping from his skin at the ear piercing yowling emanating from behind him.

"Oh," Jessie frowned, bending down to scoop up a seriously peeved black and white striped cat. "You stepped on him."

"What the hell is that?"

Jessie burst out laughing. "What do you think it is?"

"You got a cat?" Tony eyed her pet dubiously.

"He reminded me of you."

"Of me? Oh very funny." Tony snorted, giving her a mock glare. "I looked better in my stripes."

"Well, I wouldn't know. I wasn't allowed to visit."

"Ah, come on. You aren't going to hold that against me, are you?"

Jessie grinned, every care she'd had for the last several months fading into insignificance now that Tony was with her again. "I'll think about it."

Tony laughed and reached out a hesitant hand to pet the ruffled beast. The cat immediately began purring and arched into Tony's hand. Jessie knew exactly how he felt. She wanted to do the same thing.

Her cheeks burned and she bent to put the cat on the floor, hoping she'd hid the telltale blush from Tony.

"What's his name?"

"Ziggy."

Tony's incredulous laugh rang through the shop. "You named him after my cell mate?"

Jessie shrugged. "It seemed fitting."

Tony took her hand, still chuckling. "Come on doll, show me around."

She took him on a tour, showed him the expanded shop with its new deli section, and then took him to the third floor where her new apartment was getting its finishing touches.

She showed him the bedroom last. It was her favorite room. She'd had the workmen put in two large windows that flooded the room with light. Tony looked at the mattress on the floor and raised an eyebrow.

"Camping out?"

Jessie shrugged. "I couldn't wait."

"*Hmm*," he said, leaning down to steal another kiss. "I know the feeling."

She smiled, his words igniting a trail of tingling warmth that quickly spread through her, and reached up to lock her arms around his neck. "Do you now?"

"Um hmm," he murmured, walking her backward while his lips moved more urgently over hers.

When they reached the mattress, they sank down on their knees, their lips still locked together.

"I don't ever want to be away from you again," Jessie said, leaning back to give Tony better access to her neck.

He kissed his way down to her collarbone, only pausing long enough to pull her down to the mattress with him, settling over her. The warmth spread, becoming a fire she was fairly sure would melt her on the spot.

"Good to hear you say that." His lips swallowed her moan as his hands ran down her thigh. "Because you're never getting rid of me."

"Deal," Jessie said, wrapping one leg around his waist and pressing closer.

"Just one question…"

"What?" Jessie asked, her breath coming in short gasps.

"How the hell do you get these things off?"

Jessie burst out laughing and leaned up to kiss him, helping him release the buttons of her overalls while her lips drank him in.

He pulled the bib down and unbuttoned the shirt she wore beneath it, tearing his lips away from hers so he could kiss each inch of skin exposed by the buttons. When she lay bare to him, he leaned back and stared, his hungry eyes roving over her while Jessie impatiently helped him pull off his own clothing. She hadn't seen him in months, and now she couldn't get enough of him. She wanted to see *all* of him, needed to see all of him. Now.

He was everything she'd imagined and so much more. The broad lines of his shoulders bunched together as he leaned over her. Jessie reached up to run her hands down the hard planes of his stomach, her fingers twining in the dark hair sprinkled across his chest. Every inch of skin that touched hers sparked a heat that pooled low in her belly. She let her hand trail down, lower, until she brushed against the hard, solid length of him that strained toward her. Her fingers closed over him and he sucked in his breath.

Some of Jessie's nervousness dropped away at the sight of what such a small touch from her could do. This wasn't the first time she'd been with a man. But her experiences with Mario already paled in comparison. The often rushed, uncomfortable moments with him had never created the aching fire that a mere brush of Tony's hand wrought. She banished the other man from her mind, images of Tony taking their place.

Tony gently removed her hand, bringing it to his lips so he could kiss each finger in turn.

"You are unbelievably beautiful," he said, his voice breaking on the last word in a show of emotion that caused Jessie to blink back tears.

She reached up and stroked his cheek, swallowing past the lump in her throat. "You are more than I ever dreamed."

"There's been something I've been wanting to say to you for a long time now."

"Shh," Jessie murmured, pulling him down for a kiss. "You don't have to say anything."

"Yes, I do. The words have been burning on my tongue for months." He leaned down and kissed her neck, nibbling his way up to the spot just under her ear. "I love you, my beautiful Jessica," he whispered in her ear.

She smiled up at him, those tiny, simple words etching themselves into her heart and she shivered. She wrapped herself around him, snuggling as close as she could. Even a breath of air between them was too far apart for her.

He'd refused to say those words in his letters. It had frustrated her. She'd wanted to see those words written where she could read them over and over again. But the wait had been so worth it. Hearing them from his lips was pure heaven.

She laid a hand on his cheek and gently kissed his lips. "I love you so much."

He deepened their kiss, his tongue slowly exploring her mouth, tangling with her own until her head swam. She pressed closer, wrapping her arms around his shoulders to pull him against her.

He bent his head to nuzzle her neck. "I waited a long time to hear those words," he murmured. "Say them again."

She smiled, turning her head to give him better access to the tender skin beneath her ear. "I love you."

"*Hmm,*" he moaned. "Again." He nipped at her collarbone and she gasped.

"I love you, Anthony Aloysius Solomon."

Tony jerked up, horrified. "My mother told you my middle name?"

Jessie laughed. "Yes, and I love you anyway."

Tony playfully glared at her, but the expression quickly melted back into one of heated desire when she ran her palms up his bare chest.

"I love you," she said, leaning up to press a trail of kisses along his neck.

Tony groaned and ran his hand down the length of her back. She arched, pressing her heated center against the hard length of him.

He gripped her buttocks, thrusting against her, teasing her with a tiny taste and then pulling back. "Again."

"Tony?"

"*Hmm?*" he groaned.

"No more talking."

Tony chuckled and Jessie cupped his face, pulling him back to her lips.

"Your wish is my command."

He put his lips to better use, exploring the soft dips and valleys of her body while his hands played their own game along her silky skin. His palm cupped her breast, his thumb brushing across her nipple until it beaded, hard and aching. Tony's tongue flicked over it and Jessie gasped, her body arching beneath his, trying to press the tender bud closer to him. He teased her for a moment, his breath blowing across the tip until Jessie whimpered in frustration.

When his lips finally closed over it, Jessie cried out, her hands gripping his hair. His tongue swirled around the tight bead while he suckled her and Jessie threw her head back, the fire in her belly intensifying. She hadn't thought it was possible to climax from breast play alone, but Tony was about to prove her wrong.

He moved to the other breast, lavishing it with the same attention, while his hand trailed lower down her body until it found her opening, already wet and ready for him. He slid a finger inside and her hips bucked against him.

Tony groaned, adding another finger to join the first as his lips moved back up her body, his mouth once again fusing with her own.

Jessie writhed beneath him, the pressure in her core building until she wasn't sure she could stand it anymore.

"Tony!" she pleaded, no longer able to articulate what she wanted, needed, from him.

"I know, love," Tony said, moving to cover her.

He withdrew his fingers and Jessie moaned, almost sobbing at the loss.

Tony nudged her legs farther apart and she spread them eagerly to accommodate him. The hard, warm length of him pushed at her entrance and she wrapped her legs about his waist, lifting her hips to bring him closer.

Tony panted, teasing her, easing himself in slowly, an inch at a time, only to withdraw again. Jessie tossed her head from side to side, her hands clawing at the pillows beneath her.

"Tony!" she shouted again.

He chuckled, the sound full of male satisfaction, as he finally slid his full length inside her.

Jessie sucked in a ragged breath, her body stretching to adjust to him. He paused, brushing her hair back from her face, and pressed a gentle kiss on her forehead. Jessie looked into his passion-darkened eyes, and for the first time in her life, she felt whole, safe. Like she was home. Tony was her haven, her everything. And she'd never let him go again.

She moved her hips beneath him and dragged him back down to her, showing him with her lips and tongue what she wanted from him. Tony was more than happy to oblige.

He moved slowly, setting a careful rhythm that soon had Jessie crying out for more. Her legs tightened around him, her hands gripped his waist. A few more strokes and the inferno that had been building inside her finally burst, swelling through her in wave after wave of pleasure.

Tony was only a moment behind her. He arched, thrusting himself as deep as she could take him. Jessie rose up to meet him as he emptied himself into her.

He held himself still for a few moments longer, both of them enjoying the lingering ripples of their lovemaking before Tony collapsed, gently bringing her with him as he rolled to his side.

Jessie lay against Tony's chest, dragging in long, deep breaths until her heart stopped pounding. He cupped her cheek, tilting her face up so he could press a tender kiss on her lips.

"I love you," he whispered, staring deep into her eyes.

"Jailhouse cat and all?"

He chuckled, tucking her body closer to his. "Yes, cat and all."

She threaded her fingers through his and brought them up to her lips. "I love you, too."

Jessie lay in Tony's arms, happier than she had ever been in her life, her body pleasantly lethargic. She drew lazy circles through the hair on his chest.

"What's next for you?" she asked him.

"*Hmm*, well," he said, catching her hand and kissing each of her fingertips as he spoke, "first of all, I'm going to regain a little strength, and then I think I'll make love to you again." He pulled her chin toward him so he could reach her lips for a kiss. "And then again." Another kiss, longer, sweeter. "And possibly again."

Jessie laughed as his lips descended again. "I meant after, tomorrow, next week." She sobered and linked her fingers through his, laying her head back on his chest. "I know you gave up everything for me. I'm sure Jameson has made sure you'll never rejoin the force and probably ruined your P.I. business, too. I'm sorry for that."

He pulled her close. "None of that is your fault, nothing to be sorry for. I actually thought I might try my hand at being a butcher."

Jessie looked up at him, happiness flowing through her. "You want to work with me?"

He shrugged. "I thought I might be good at it. I did a pretty fine job when I helped with the orphanage delivery."

"Yes, you did." She kissed him, letting her lips linger on his. "I'd love to have you at the shop."

"Well, that's settled then." He propped the arm that wasn't holding Jessie behind his head and stared at the recessed ceiling Jessie had had the workers create in this room. "You've done a beautiful job with this place."

"Thank you," Jessie said, inordinately pleased that he liked it.

"What will be on the second floor?"

Jessie blushed. She wished she'd had a little warning that he was coming so she could have figured out what to say. What if he didn't want the same thing she did? To have her building renovated around plans for a future that he might not share had been crazy. Yet she couldn't imagine a future without him. Though, since he wanted to work with her, and after the passion they had just shared, she hoped perhaps he had the same idea for their future as she did.

"Oh come on, it can't be that bad," he said, chuckling. "Unless…please tell me you aren't planning on installing a new speakeasy in here."

Jessie laughed. "No! Nothing like that. I thought…well, I thought that if you got out and were still interested, still wanted, I mean, to be with me…I thought that your mother might like to come live here. With us. So I had them install a second apartment and I figured she wouldn't want to climb too many stairs so the second floor would be ideal…"

Tony stared at her, his mouth hanging open for a moment before he snapped it shut.

"If you had other plans, or if this isn't what you want—"

Tony's lips silenced anything else she was going to say.

"I love you so much," he said, kissing her again. "You are an amazing, generous, incredible woman."

He crushed her to him, sitting up so he could pull her fully into his arms. He brought his hands up to cup her face. She smiled at him through the tears that suddenly threatened to spill over. Again. She'd turned into a complete crybaby since she'd fallen in love with him, but she couldn't help it. The emotions she'd spent a lifetime keeping contained couldn't seem to be controlled when she was around him.

She gazed into the eyes of the man she loved more than the air she breathed. "I thought my life was over, the night the shop burned down. I lost everything. I lost you."

"Your life is *not* over. I won't allow anyone to take anything else from you ever again."

Jessie gave him a small smile. "So you're going to protect me from the whole world now?"

He smiled back and kissed the tip of her nose. "I love you, Jessie. You are *mine*. No one is going to take you away from me. I will protect you from anyone and anything that so much as puts a frown on your beautiful face."

Jessie's heart nearly burst from the sheer ecstasy that flooded it and she rose up to meet his lips again. "I love you too, Tony."

"Jessica Harlan, you have turned my world upside down. I've thought of you every moment since the day I met you and I don't ever want to let you go. Will you marry me?"

"Yes." Jessie smiled, answering almost before he'd finished asking. Her laugh ended with a joyful sob. "Yes, yes, yes." She threw her arms around his neck and kissed him until her head began to spin.

"You sure you want to spend the rest of your life here with me?" she murmured against his lips.

"I can't imagine spending it anywhere else."

"Shall we drink to it?" Jessie asked.

Tony looked at her, horrified, and Jessie burst out laughing. "I'm just teasing."

"Oh, funny. You just slay me."

Jessie laughed again and snuggled against him. "I never thought I'd find it, you know."

"Find what?"

"Someone I could trust, someone I loved, who loved me. Something real."

Tony put a finger under her chin and raised her face so he could look into her eyes. "I know how you feel." He stroked his thumb across her cheek. "But I think we found it, baby. The real McCoy."

"I think we did," Jessie said. She kissed him and then leaned back, her head cocked to the side. "Tony?"

"Yes, doll?"

"Will you sing for me?"

Tony's laughter rang out. "Anything for you, doll."

Jessie grinned into the darkness, letting Tony's surprisingly beautiful voice wash over her, and thanked her lucky stars that she'd get to keep an eye on the handsome Mr. Solomon for the rest of her life.

A dirty job to be sure…and she was just the gal to do it.

BONUS CONTENT

Tony and Jessie's Letters

April 22, 1928

Dear Tony,

I hope this note finds you in good health and spirits…and soon to be released. Surely, even a man as pigheaded as Agent Jameson will relent in his revenge soon. You were right. I went to him and made the deal. Turned over everything I had on the Phoenix and in exchange, I've got my freedom. I tried to bargain for yours, as well, but I'm sure you can imagine how that went. Still, he can't leave you in there for long. There is no reason, now that he's got everything he needs on the Phoenix.

Though, truth be told, if you weren't just as pigheaded as Jameson, you wouldn't be cooling your heels in that box. I am filled with both guilt and anger that you are stuck in that joint. Guilt because I hate to see you in that place, knowing it is because of me. And anger because you took all this upon yourself without even discussing it with me! You silly, stubborn man, I don't know what you were thinking!

Mostly, I am filled with concern for you. Are they treating you well? Is there anything I can do? I so wish we'd had more time the other day, as there are many things we need to say. I look forward to continuing our conversation in person. I will come to see you soon.

Best regards,
Jessica

April 25, 1928

Dear Jessica,

I hope this letter finds you well. I must warn you, I've always been a stubborn mule, as I am sure my mother will attest. It is important that you understand this, because I intend to be around to plague you with my various faults for a very long time. Best you get used to them now. As for your inquiry, my thoughts on my actions were simple...I'd much rather be in here than see you in this place.

And on that subject, please do not worry for me. It's really not so bad, aside from my cell mate's propensity for snoring, which keeps me awake until the wee hours of the morning. Then again, I fill those hours thinking of you. So all in all, I consider it time well spent.

As for being released soon, having known Jameson a good number of years longer than you, I have no doubt he will exact his revenge for as long as possible. But have no fear; even he can't keep me in here forever.

I am also looking forward to continuing our conversation in person, as well as continuing another activity that we've barely had the time to begin. But I must ask that you don't visit me again. I will look forward to your letters and to the day when I can see you again with great anticipation...but I do not want it to be in this place. This is no place for you. It is no place for the things I wish to say to you. I want our relationship built on a foundation that doesn't include bars. Or horizontal black stripes. My navy pinstripe looks much better on me.

How are you? Write me soon.

Tony

April 29, 1928

Dear Tony,

I am fine, thank you. Work has begun on the new shop and I have some plans for a modest expansion. My arm is healing, though the skin is still tender. My doctor assures me it will be right as rain soon, but I will most likely bear some scars. I'm trying not to dwell on that.

I hope that you are wrong about Jameson; however, I fear you'll be proved right. And on that note, what do you mean by asking me not to visit? We have no idea how long Jameson will drag this out. What if you are in there for weeks or even months? If you intend to be around for a very long time, as you say, then why on earth should your surroundings matter? I don't care where you are, or for that matter, what you are wearing (except I will agree that your navy pinstripe looks quite nice on you).

I'll give you fair warning. I can be every bit as stubborn as you. And I have the added advantage of having my freedom. If you don't want to see me, well then perhaps I'll just have a little chat with your cell mate. I'm sure he'd at least appreciate my company.

I will see you soon,

Jessie

May 1, 1928

Dear Jessie,

I am very happy to hear that things are going well. I have no doubt your new shop will be the toast of the town. I am even happier to hear about your arm. Don't worry about scars. They only prove that you were stronger than something that tried to hurt you. Wear them proudly.

As for my insistence on not receiving visitors, you aren't going to change my mind on that point, though I'm flattered you find me irresistible in my navy pinstripe. I hope you believe that I'd like nothing more than the pleasure of your company. But not here. I have my reasons for wanting you to keep away. My cell mate Ziggy, (as I've taken to calling him since it fits him much better than his real name, Bartholomew), would probably be more than happy to visit with you, but I wouldn't recommend it. The man speaks only in incoherent mumbles and his hygiene leaves much to be desired.

I promise you, when we finally meet again, the wait will be worth the while. There are a few things we've only just started that I have every intention of finishing. But I don't want you in this place, around these criminals. We will see each other soon.

Trust in me,
Tony

May 3, 1928

Dear Mr. Solomon,

I don't know if I have ever been so angry in all my days. You refuse to see me? I travel all the way to the jailhouse just to be told that you aren't accepting visitors? I have half a mind to come back and request to visit Ziggy. It would serve you right.

Miss Jessica Harlan

P.S. I don't recall using the word "irresistible" when discussing your navy pinstripe. And those "things" you intend on finishing? Well, you can just go ahead and finish them by yourself.

May 7, 1928

My darling Jessie,

Come on, doll. Don't be so angry. You know it's for the best. I don't think you realize what a good opportunity we've got here. We've got a chance to really get to know each other without all the…shall we say *distractions* that always seem to arise when we are together. So let's not waste it. There are so many things I want to know about you. I've got nothing but time here and reading material is nonexistent. So tell me everything. What's your favorite color? Favorite food? What was your childhood like working in the butcher shop with your pop? I want to know everything.

Thinking of you,
Tony

P.S. While I could, I suppose, handle those matters I mentioned on my own, it would be much more pleasurable for us both if I waited until we were together again. I promise you.

May 10, 1928

Dear Tony,

I still haven't forgiven you, but in the interest of doing my Christian duty to help poor, unfortunate wretches such as yourself, I'll answer your questions. There's really not much to tell. My life is rather boring. It's always revolved around the shop and now that other matters have been resolved, the shop is my focus again. Speaking of which, it's coming together nicely. I have walls! My apartment isn't quite ready yet, but I'll be moving back in just as soon as it is. Maude has been a doll putting me up, but she's getting ready for her big June wedding and the last thing she needs is a permanent houseguest.

To answer your questions, my favorite color is green. My favorite food is bread. Any kind. All kinds. Can't get enough of the stuff, which is unfortunate for my waistline. As for my childhood, it was wonderful. Unique, I suppose. I don't really remember much of my life before the orphanage. Just flashes every now and then. What I remember most was being cold, and hungry. Always cold and hungry.

The smell of lavender reminds me of my mother. I can't really remember her face anymore. Someone asked me once if I was angry with her for abandoning me. I was. For a long time. I wanted to know why she'd leave me. I wish I could remember. And at the same time I'm thankful I can't.

When I do think of her, the memories are coated in sadness. I don't think she wanted to give me up. I think she may have been sick, because sometimes I wake at night with the echo of long ago coughing and retching ringing in my head. And in all my vague memories, there is never anyone but my mother. Perhaps she was ill and couldn't care for me. I don't know. It doesn't matter, I suppose. All I know is I'd never abandon a child of mine. But then again, a tiny part of me fears that maybe, if I'd been in whatever situation she'd found herself in, maybe I would.

In time though, I grew grateful to her for the choice she made. It brought me to my father. I know there was a fuss about him adopting me. A single man adopting a young female? I don't know that it had ever been done before. To be honest, I'm still not sure how many palms he greased to swing it. I'm glad he did. He never told me why he chose me. All he ever said was it was fate. I think it might have been the bread.

When he was making one of his meat deliveries to the orphanage, he'd left the door to the truck cab open, and there was a basket from the bakery, brimming full of fresh baked bread. I knew it was for the orphanage, and I'd get a piece with my dinner. But I just couldn't resist. I darted in, grabbed a loaf and took off running. He caught up with me in an alley a block away. There I was just stuffing my face as fast as I could. I remember him staring down at me, and I was afraid I'd get in trouble. But he just watched me for a second and then left. A few months later, he took me home. I was eight.

Life with my pop was happy. I'd go to school and then help him in the shop. I'd watch him fiddling with his stills while he sang at the top of his lungs. He couldn't hit a note to save his life, but he sure enjoyed trying. On Sundays, he'd take me on picnics in the park or sometimes we'd go to the bakery of a friend of his and I'd sit and the baker's wife and I would make all kinds of goodies while Pop and his friends would play cards. Life was grand. I miss him.

And the rest, you know. Now it's your turn. Spill it.

Thinking of you, too,
Jessie

P.S. Promises, promises. I suppose we'll just have to wait and see.

May 14, 1928

Dear Jessie,

Your father sounds like he was a wonderful man. I wish I could have met him. My childhood wasn't unique in any way. Well, I was an only child, so I was probably a bit spoiled. My ma made sure I minded my manners though. And she taught me to cook. I can whip up a mean pile of pasta. And a chocolate soufflé that you'd sell your soul for. Just don't spread that around. I've got a reputation to protect.

I am sorry for the pain you went through when you were young. For what it's worth, I have no doubt that you'd find a way to make it through, no matter what your circumstances. I've never met anyone as strong, determined, and just plain stubborn as you are. And I know you will make an amazing mother.

I'm glad you were able to find happiness with your father. If I ever get out of this joint, (and there are days where I'm starting to think Jameson will never give up), it will be my very great pleasure to make sure there is always a smile on your beautiful face. You'll just have to allow me. That stubborn streak I mentioned you have? Not always a good thing. (I say this with a smile but only partially in jest.)

It's time for lights out, so I must go. It's my favorite part of the day. Eight whole hours of lying in the dark and dreaming of you. There are definitely worse ways to spend my time.

Dreaming of you through the night and during the day,
Tony

P.S. I never make a promise I can't keep.

May 17, 1928

Dear Tony,

All right, upon leaving that godforsaken hole you are in, you must come immediately to my shop…and make me a chocolate soufflé! You have my mouth absolutely watering. I mentioned it to your mother the other day (I've been making a point of visiting her once a week so we can compare letters. We are both missing you dreadfully), and ever since, she has done nothing but rave about your culinary prowess. I'm not sure I'm convinced. Mothers' opinions of their children are always a bit biased.

I am *not* stubborn! Well, no more so than the average person, I don't think. I do appreciate your faith in me. I'm not always so sure, myself.

Wonderful news! The shop is finished enough that I can move back in! There is still a lot of work to be done, of course, but the walls are up, the plumbing is working, and I can live there! Maude has been an absolute doll for letting me stay with her, but I'm used to having my own space. And it's a joy to be back at the shop. I thought I'd lost it for good. I know it won't ever be the same, but I'm grateful to have it back.

Speaking of work to be done, I must be off. I think I might stop in and see Jameson again. This has gone past vindictive and into the realm of insanity.

Dreaming of you, too, every night,
Jessie

P.S. Well, since I haven't known you for long, I'll have to take your word for it. Just what exactly are you promising anyway? You have me curious.

May 22, 1928

Dear Jessie,

That is wonderful news! I'm so happy to hear it. I can't wait to see your new place. Having said that, however, I'd rather you don't visit Jameson again. The man is a stubborn ass and on him it's not nearly as attractive as it is on you. I've spoken with my lawyer and he feels I'll be released soon. Jameson has no reason to hold me any longer and he knows it.

Ziggy and I have had a falling out. A small misunderstanding over bunk territory. I emerged victorious and I'm afraid Ziggy wasn't happy with the outcome. No matter. I prefer the silence over his incoherent chatter.

It eases my mind tremendously to know you are keeping an eye on my mother for me. And I'm sure she has only told you the absolute truth about me. I can't help it if I'm a perfect specimen of a man. A fact I will be most happy to prove to you when I see you next.

Perfectly yours,
Tony

P.S. I promise that the next time I see you, I will continue what we began in my car and in my office. And I promise you that next time <u>nothing</u> will interrupt us. I'd be a little more explicit but I'd rather my mother not see it. Or Ziggy. He's currently looking over my shoulder.

May 27, 1928

Dear Tony,

I still think a visit to Jameson might help speed things along a bit. Maybe if I make a big nuisance of myself, he'll have to let you go. Nonetheless, I'll agree to stay away from him for the simple reason that I loathe the man. I greatly look forward to the day when we can be rid of him for good.

I am sorry you and Ziggy aren't getting along, though you will be happy to know that your mother is doing splendidly. Maude and I took her to the beauty salon a few days ago and we are all looking quite dapper, if I do say so myself. Afterwards, she made us a simply mouthwatering chicken parmesan. She says you make it better. I don't believe her. You'll have to make it for me when you get out, so I can judge properly.

Also, a belated condolence on the loss of your beloved Chauncey. Though why a ten-year-old boy would be so fond of a cockroach is beyond me. I regret to inform you, however, that your mother confessed. She squashed him with a shoe and did not send him to live with your aunt in Iowa. I am also very sorry to hear that you were teased so mercilessly by the boys in your neighborhood for having daily tea parties with your cousin Gertie. I think it was a lovely thing to do.

I will write more later, but I must run now. I want to catch the post before it goes, and I need to be here when my new shop sign arrives!

Affectionately yours,
Jessie

P.S. As you were so kind in detailing your promises, I'll make one of my own. I promise to make sure you make good on your promises. I also promise to make sure the door is locked.

P.P.S. I'd never show anything so personal to your mother!

P.P.P.S. Please send my regards to Ziggy.

May 31, 1928

Dearest Jessie,

    I can't tell you how happy it makes me to hear of your outings with my mother. Though I'm terrified about what else she might be telling you. For one thing, I did NOT have tea parties with Gertie. We only pretended to have tea parties so we could sneak a swig of her father's whiskey and no one would be the wiser. I am devastated to hear of the true demise of Chauncey. I should have known something was fishy. I always did wonder how a cockroach could make it to Iowa all on his own.

    Thank you for taking such good care of my mother. While I can't imagine the beauty parlor being able to improve upon any of your looks, I'm sure you all dolled up gorgeously. And congratulations on the sign! I can't wait to see it.

    I'm afraid I must cut this letter short. I only have a few minutes. I have a meeting with my lawyer. I hope this mess will be cleared up soon and I'll be on my way to you.

    Yours always,
    Tony

    P.S. Locking the door...now why didn't I ever think of that?

    P.P.S. Ziggy is flattered you remembered him. He says hello.

June 4, 1928

Tony! That's wonderful. How did the meeting go? What happened? What did your lawyer say? Will you be coming home soon? Your mother and I are beside ourselves. Please hurry and write and give us the news!!

Anxiously yours,
Jessie

P.S. Ah, I think I'm getting rather fond of Ziggy. Hello back to him.

June 7, 1928

My dearest Jessie,

I hope you will forgive me if I wax a little lyrical for a moment. Ziggy has been removed for the time being, and for the first time since being here, I find myself alone. Sitting on the top bunk, I can see the sky through the window in my cell. It's about to storm, I think. The sun is shining, but you can't see it through the haze of the overcast sky. It's just bright enough to turn the sky that beautiful blue gray that precedes a good rain.

It's the same color as your eyes when you are in my arms. When they have darkened with the passion we've stoked between us. I love that shade of blue. I told you before my favorite color is green, but I don't think that is the case any longer. No, my new favorite color is the blue gray of the sky before a storm. Of your eyes when I've kissed you until you tremble in my arms.

You are, quite literally, my everything. You are my life now, the reason I get out of bed every morning. Your face fills my mind every waking moment of the day, and of the night. I want nothing more than to get out of this box and show you every day, for the rest of my life, how much you mean to me. I have never felt so strongly about anyone before. Ever. I never knew it was even possible to feel this way about someone. Not until I met you. I will never be able to express how much you mean to me, though I plan on spending a lifetime trying.

There's something I've wanted to say to you for a while now. Something I never thought I'd say to any woman. But I won't say it just yet. Not in a letter sent from a prison. The first time you hear those words from me, I will be a free man, with a future to offer you. And you will be in my arms, those big blue eyes of yours looking right into mine, so I can be sure that you hear and understand exactly what those words mean to me, what you mean to me.

The meeting with my lawyer went very well. I should be home soon. Keep waiting for me, my love. I'll be there soon. I promise.

Yours, forever and always,
Tony

POPULAR PROHIBITION ERA COCKTAILS

Bee's Knees

1½ oz. gin
1 tsp. honey
1 tsp. fresh lemon juice
Ice

Combine all ingredients in a shaker. Shake, strain into a chilled coupe glass and garnish with a twist of lemon.

Source—https://imbibemagazine.com/Bee-s-Knees

Brandy Crusta

This classic cocktail was originally made with Cognac but can also be made with brandy, bourbon or rye whiskey. It's also one of the few cocktails that you garnish before making the drink.

2 oz. cognac
1 tsp. orange curacao
½ tsp. fresh lemon juice
1 dash Angostura bitters
Crushed ice

Cut a lemon in half. Pare the full peel off half and squeeze the juice from the lemon. Prepare a cocktail glass by moistening the rim with lemon and dipping it in sugar, then carefully curling the lemon peel around the inside of a glass. Combine all ingredients in a shaker, shake and strain into glass and add 1 small cube of ice.

Adapted from Vintage Spirits & Forgotten Cocktails *by Ted Haigh*

Source—http://imbibemagazine.com/Recipe-Brandy-Crusta

Dubonnet Cocktail

1 shot gin
1 shot Dubonnet
Lemon twist

Add a few ice cubes to a mixing glass. Add Dubonnet and gin. Mix and strain into a chilled cocktail or rock glass. Garnish with a twist of lemon.

Source—www.theframedtable.com/2013/08/gin-dubonnet-cocktail

Highball

1 shot rye whisky
Ginger ale

Add ice to a highball glass. Mix in ingredients. Serve.

Source - http://www.chiff.com/a/mixed-drinks.htm

French 45

1 oz. gin or cognac
½ oz. Cointreau liqueur
½ oz. lemon juice
Champagne

Pour the lemon juice, gin, and Cointreau into a cocktail shaker with ice cubes. Shake well. Strain well into a chilled champagne flute. Carefully fill with champagne.

Source—www.cocktails.about.com/od/atozcocktailrecipes/r/frnch_75_cktl.htm

The Last Word

¼ cup gin
2 Tbs. Chartreuse liqueur
2 Tbs. fresh lime juice
2 Tbs. maraschino liqueur (such as Luxardo)
2 lime twists

Pour gin, Chartreuse, lime juice, and maraschino liqueur into a cocktail shaker. Add ice; cover and shake vigorously ten times. Strain into two chilled coupe or martini glasses. Garnish each with a twist of lime.

Source—www.bonappetit.com/recipe/the-last-word

The Southside
Rumored to be Al Capone's favorite drink

2 oz. gin
1 oz. simple syrup
¾ oz. fresh lime juice
3-4 oz. soda water
2 mint sprigs
2 pieces lime

Muddle one sprig of mint with the lime pieces, lime juice, and simple syrup in the bottom of a bar glass. Add gin and shake well. Pour into a goblet over crushed ice and stir until the outer-glass frosts. Top with soda water, garnish with remaining sprig of mint, and serve.

Source—www.drinksmixer.com/drink7454.html

The Side Car

¾ oz. Cointreau
¾ oz. lemon juice
1½ oz. cognac

Shake well with cracked ice, then strain into a chilled cocktail glass that has had its outside rim rubbed with lemon juice and dipped in sugar.

Source—www.esquire.com/drinks/sidecar-drink-recipe

Mary Pickford

1.5 oz. white rum
1.5 oz. pineapple juice
1 tsp. grenadine
6 drops maraschino liqueur

Add all the ingredients to a cocktail shaker and fill with ice. Shake, and strain into a chilled cocktail glass.

Source—www.liquor.com/recipes/mary-pickford/

Tuxedo #2

2 oz. gin
¾ oz. dry vermouth
¼ oz. maraschino liqueur
2 dashes orange bitters
Absinthe rinse

Combine ingredients (except absinthe) in a chilled mixing glass and stir with ice for 15 seconds. Rinse the inside of a chilled cocktail glass with Absinthe and then discard the excess. Strain stirred ingredients into chilled coupe and serve. Garnish with a lemon twist.

Source—www.foodrepublic.com/2012/03/22/tuxedo-no-2-cocktail

Ward 8

2 oz. rye or bourbon
½ oz. freshly squeezed lemon juice
½ oz. freshly squeezed orange juice
1 tsp. grenadine
Ice
1 maraschino cherry

Fill a cocktail glass with ice and place in the freezer to chill. Place the rye or bourbon, lemon juice, orange juice, and grenadine in a cocktail shaker. Fill the shaker halfway with ice and shake vigorously until the outside is frosty, about 30 seconds. Strain into the chilled glass and garnish with the maraschino cherry.

Source—www.chow.com/recipes/10361-ward-eight

Bacardi Cocktail

3 oz. Bacardi Superior Rum
2 oz. fresh lime juice
¼ oz. sugar
1 oz. grenadine

Add all the ingredients to a shaker and fill with ice. Shake, and strain into a cocktail glass.

Source—www.iquor.com/recipes/bacardi-cocktail-2/

12 Mile Limit

1 oz. silver rum
½ oz. rye whiskey
½ oz. brandy
½ oz. grenadine
½ oz. fresh lemon juice
1 lemon twist, to garnish

Combine rum, whiskey, brandy, grenadine, and juice in a cocktail shaker filled with ice; cover and shake until chilled, about 15 seconds. Strain into a chilled highball glass and top with lemon twist.

Source—www.saveur.com/article/Recipes/Classic-12-Mile-Limit-Cocktail

The White Lady

2 oz. gin
½ oz. Cointreau
½ oz. lemon juice
1 egg white

Shake well with cracked ice, then strain into a chilled cocktail glass.

Source—www.esquire.com/drinks/white-lady-drink-recipe

Acknowledgments

A huge thanks to my amazing editor, Erin Molta. I don't know what I, or my books, would do without you. To my whole team at Entangled, especially Gwen Hayes, Heidi Stryker, Debbie Suzuki, and Nancy Cantor, thank you so much for all you do. Babs Hightower, thank you for everything! To Toni Kerr, Cole Gibsen, and Lisa Amowitz, the best group of friends, motivators, and cheerleaders any writer could ask for, thank you! A special thanks to Kristal Shaff—without your much-needed nagging and our writing sprint sessions this book would probably never have gotten done. I look forward to returning the favor. And as always, my eternal love and thanks to my amazing family. You guys keep me going when nothing else does, you support me no matter what, you patiently dig your clothes out of baskets every morning and never complain when I say, "I just need one more minute." Tom, Connor, and Ryanna—you are my life. Mike and Laurie Marquis, you are seriously the world's best parents; Jeanette, Ryan and Gail, Shaun and Michelle, Brandon and Shannon, Matt and Mindy, Kyelie and Andy—thank you all for your love and support!

About the Author

Romance and non-fiction author Michelle McLean is a jeans and t-shirt kind of girl who is addicted to chocolate and Goldfish crackers and spent most of her formative years with her nose in a book. She has a B.S. in History, a M.A. in English, and loves her romance with a hearty side of suspenseful mystery.

When Michelle's not editing, reading or chasing her kids around, she can usually be found in a quiet corner working on her next book. She resides in PA with her husband and two children, an insanely hyper dog, and three very spoiled cats.

Michelle loves to hear from her readers—you can email her at authormichellemclean@yahoo.com, leave a review at any site that sells her books, or find her at her blog, on Facebook, and at Twitter.

Get Scandalous with these historical reads...

LOVE'S REVENGE
a *Worth Brothers'* novel by Joan Avery

St. Louis, Missouri, 1879

The only things that have kept widower Stephen Worth alive for the past two years are the promise of revenge against the man who framed him for murder and the love for Andy, his son, who was taken by the beautiful but vexing sister of his dead wife. Now, full of desire for her, he must convince Kate to trust him before she learns the truth about his past—but his demons are all the ammunition she needs to keep his son for good.

ONCE UPON A MASQUERADE
a novel by Tamara Hughes

NEW YORK CITY, 1883

Self-made shipping magnate Christopher Black first spies Rebecca Bailey at a masquerade ball and is captivated by her refreshing naïveté and sparkling beauty. But when Christopher's investigation of the murder of his best friend leads him straight to Rebecca, he fears his ingénue may be a femme fatale in disguise. Now he must decide if he can trust the woman he's come to love, or if her secrets will be his downfall.

THE EARL'S WAGER
a *Reluctant Bride* novel by Rebecca Thomas

When straight laced earl, Will Sutton, is challenged to turn an obstinate American ward, Miss Georgia Duvall, into a biddable lady suitable for the Marriage Mart, he gladly takes the wager. Then has to decide whether the prize—a prime racing stud horse—is worth changing the impudent beauty's temperament he's come to enjoy. Greatly.

Made in the USA
Monee, IL
11 January 2022

88673634R00152